F. N. Otieno is a Kenyan language student in Munich, Germany, and an aspiring writer, poet, and a playwright, greatly passionate about literature. Her work entails quite catchy literary style, expressions and creativity in the topic. With this, the readers are assured an enjoyable and educational experience. Her first showcased dramatised poem, *The Lady's Handbag*, earned her a Certificate of Merit during the Athi River District 2014 Kenya Drama Festivals. She also has an interest in culture, art and dance, as well as learning new languages. She is currently studying the German language.

To my motivators.

F. N. Otieno

SHAKESPEARE'S ROMEO AND JULIET

THE SEQUEL AND TWELVE TALES

AUSTIN MACAULEY PUBLISHERS™
LONDON · CAMBRIDGE · NEW YORK · SHARJAH

Copyright © F. N. Otieno (2019)

The right of F. N. Otieno to be identified as author of this work has been asserted by her in accordance with section 77 and 78 of the Copyright, Designs and Patents Act 1988.

All rights reserved. No part of this publication may be reproduced, stored in a retrieval system or transmitted in any form or by any means, electronic, mechanical, photocopying, recording or otherwise, without the prior permission of the publishers.

Any person who commits any unauthorised act in relation to this publication may be liable to criminal prosecution and civil claims for damages.

A CIP catalogue record for this title is available from the British Library.

ISBN 9781788486149 (Paperback)
ISBN 9781788486156 (Hardback)
ISBN 9781528954600 (ePub e-book)

www.austinmacauley.com

First Published (2019)
Austin Macauley Publishers Ltd
25 Canada Square
Canary Wharf
London
E14 5LQ

I would like to acknowledge Austin Macauley publishing group with gratitude for providing a platform to begin my writing career and selecting my manuscript as one worth publishing and presentable to readers, as well as the designers, editors and the production management for shaping and making the production of the book possible from the top cover to the great appealing presentation of the book. I'd like to thank the marketing staff for ensuring the effective distribution of the work to the surface for all my readers.

I give great gratitude to my mother and sister, who sacrificed financially to contribute to the publication of the book. Also, Angila, and relatives that took part in funding the manuscript, as well as my family for their wonderful encouragement and inspiration during my writing process. I would lastly like to give acknowledgement to Christine for the effective and productive training of my language skills as a student and a potential aspiring write, and to all my readers who share in the appreciation of my work.

Synopsis

Shakespeare's *Romeo and Juliet: The Sequel and Twelve Tales* is a collection of stories that explore the dark and ironic part of life that we only tend to fancy through the lives of these extraordinary characters. The stories *Death and the Peasant*, *John Cooper's Casket* and *The Author's Authentic Disease* are based on the theme of grim death circumstances in which the characters face different faces of what a person could imagine as death or haunted experience. *Teles* and *Harvey's Honeymoon* are stories that put love in very dangerous grounds. *Teles* describes a sailor's undiluted love for a mythical creature, a sea nymph who becomes his end. *Harvey's Honeymoon* describes a couple's horrid choice of a honeymoon in the skirts of an untamed place chained with many horrific events. *The Confession* is a story about the confession of a reckless superior with a disorder that drives him to purge terror upon his subjects. *Behind the Red Door* is a haunted story of a tormented human spirit in the hands of witchery. Shakespeare's *Romeo and Juliet: Fancies of Friar Laurence* is a fantastic sequel of Shakespeare's *Romeo and Juliet* that goes further to illustrate the ability of pure love to suppress even the ends of existence, death. Friar Laurence the priestly character who weds the late couples is, a year after their death, put to take part in a dreamy desperate quest of reviving their grieving souls in the spiritual love for each other.

Table of Contents

Chapter 1 — 13
Death and the Peasant 'Tale Between Man and Death'

Chapter 2 — 17
Harvey's Honeymoon 'Tale of Love on Haunted Grounds'

Chapter 3 — 24
Behind the Red Door 'Struggles of a Psychotic Mind'

Chapter 4 — 30
Teles 'Tragic Love Story'

Chapter 5 — 37
Declarations of Love 'A Certain Dream'

Chapter 6 — 41
The Author's Authentic Disease 'A Strange Edge of an Author'

Chapter 7 — 48
Shakespeare's Romeo and Juliet: The Sequel Fancies of Friar Laurence 'A Tale from a Once-Existing Love'

Chapter 8 — 58
Odds of Benevilla 'Facts of a Town'

Chapter 9 — 61
The Confession 'Confessions of a Superior'

Chapter 10 67

The Casket of John Cooper 'Tale of Grim Death'

Chapter 11 75

Guilt of Killing 'A Murder Case'

Chapter 1
Death and the Peasant
'Tale Between Man and Death'

Death is not good. Death is not bad. Death is neutral. Death does what it was born to do on earth.

In the lingering chills of the approaching night and feeble gleams of the moonlight, the thick misty fog clouded the damp air from the earth. A poor peasant man had already made his way to the town's old cemetery in such an obvious case of mourning and paying respect to his deceased daughter and wife, as the evening drew on. Died six months ago as a result of famine. They had lest to eat and too weak to beg. No plague would have done it better than to fell a life or lives from poor families. A great catastrophe that aroused merciless horror. A sickening of the heart.

The sense of sufferable gloom pervaded his drowned spirit all the way to their graves. "Oh dear, life has reclaimed thee unfairly. Oh, what am I left with if not scares of rotted away now illegitimate corpses? Souls of no more belonging." He sobbed, his lips somewhat thin and pallid. The peasant distinctly remembered the core of sorrow tapping at his cottage door only to bring demise at his doorstep. Only that and nothing more, like an obligation, a sacrifice. "Why not I coffined six feet under the ground?" he lamented.

Everything in his sight had become oppressive, even the odours of the flowers were oppressive, his eyes tortured by even a faint light. Slowly, the night approached in a ghastly pallor with lingering chills. The ebon blackness of the night dint shakes the peasant. He only stood to his feet and started narrating from the fading sound in his heart.

> *Once in a dark past*
> *A past where torment raged*
> *Stabbing the back repeatedly until I pondered*
> *Weak and weary, the deliverer of doom*
> *Cast into a dark paradise*
> *I stood there cold and frozen*
> *I slept there hungry with dreams unsuitable for mortals*
> *And the end of it I hoped, hoped for a beam of light*
> *I wake up again expecting shimmers and shine*
> *Oh, what tragedy I still find*
> *I am enveloped in pain and loss*
> *Wait, a minute*
> *Let me embrace my life*
> *As if there was something worth embracing*
> *In this surface of gloom and doom.*

In the midst of his narration, a sudden voice that could strike the earth barren veered in the damp air from trunks of decayed trees, surrounding a tarnished stone statue. "Now what do you gain weeping out all your tears?"

The peasant stared around seemingly at nothing and asked, "And whom must you be less concerned about my grief? Do I not delight in a more pitiful state?"

"I am Death," replied the voice.

The peasant became terrified, but he was beyond that. Life only inspired him with horror. He couldn't grapple with the shadowy fancies that crowded upon him as he pondered. Throwing himself helplessly on the gravel, he cried, "If so your name, then you have deprived mine from me to just but a pounding dog in the skirts of a world I hold no worth."

"No, it is false. I only respond to a mortal's fate. It's like a sentence passed in the court of law. What is foretold is done. I only happen to execute a life sentenced to me."

An air of stern, deep and irredeemable gloom hung over him emphasising his loneliness and nothingness.

"Look, dearest, why not perish and be lost?" the voice spoke and the peasant responded.

"And what right do you have to say it?"

"You live in an atmosphere which at all has no infinity with the air of heaven. Believe me, you'll find better peace with what I have in mind," Death said persuasively. He began to narrate again:

Rodents won't stop pestering me
Stealing a tiny pot of corn to last me four days
Birds no longer flee near my residence as a sign of hope
Shadows creep around my bed and with them comes
misfortunes
Oooh! Curses!
I sweat blood yet no harvest
No offspring to invite me home
Nor consort to mend my wounds
Oooh! What deplore

The tension had become like a pestilent mystic vapour, dull, sluggish and faintly discernable. "Tell me, Death, where do you take the dead?" he asked.

"I take them to find rest. Are you yet not too blind to see the sun?"

"Yes, I see the sun which only burns my skin in deceit, mercilessly to one with no cream, with many sores and pores with purse."

The voice proceeded, "The sun rises at dawn and sets at dusk. Its light only brings life on the day and takes it away as it sets. But where they go has a light that never fades nor trees that shade."

The peasant stared down.

"This world cannot favour all men, you know."

"No man is favoured by the world, his heart must grieve and hands bleed to mould fine clay," the deathly voice spoke honestly. They all had stories to tell unhidden of their success. A bit enlightened, the peasant stood and let out a grim smile. He lifted both hands up to the dark skies.

Of course, I can be
The tenor of riches
The wizard of wishes
Pledge to the agony I have been
Rather broken and torn
But of course, I can be
No longer a rat but instead a bird
That I shall fly both day and night
In which way I wish.

"Yet, passes the man and back remains the gold. Trained I am to kill without cautious, craft the drift between him and whatever he holds sacred on the land called *'earth'* only rented to man as a temporary lodging," Death said to him. The urge to persuade the peasant to give in rattled. With its voice cold and relentless in his eardrums, it seemed quite a push to him. No more could he take it. Barely able to relieve the dark past and tormenting screams at his crib. Strangled by the gravity of death, the poor old man lay flat in the dirt in surrender and death passed him in a strong gust of wind.

Chapter 2
Harvey's Honeymoon
'Tale of Love on Haunted Grounds'

Strange, I thought, how you could be living your dreams and your nightmares at the very same time.
—*Ransom Riggs*

At the occurrence of a wedding, feeling the musical realm illuminating the air with the air of love, unending laughter, and applaud. And so, it seemed as Harvey Brooklyn and Mary nay Benet made their vows of total love and commitment till death do them part. And so, it was the time it lasted, embedded in each other's love and flares. As the process goes on awaiting the couples' supreme retreat, the honeymoon. In secret planning the foundation of their home in the near future. The venue was a rare stage, unlikely to spend a honeymoon for fun-loving newlyweds. It was more of a thrilling chiller joint at the far north of Rose Bell City, The Grim Hotel where the young couple's enthusiasm adapted to suit them.

Within the ghastly feared forest of riddles with which the night arose, strongly conveying the miserable dark leaves and humongous tree trunks clash against one another in fury by the chilling gust of wind. Hardly would the sun or moon penetrate its light rays past the tip of the forest's vast expanse. It was dark to the point of evoking fear. They didn't bother, however, riding and twisting through the dark daunting woods unaided by least a warden to their destination.

Their progress arrested beneath some folds of rock layers surrounding the remarkable hotel. By the view, you could tell it's nothing ever seen in the city. There was silence, total silence, black and void like no trace of existence as the receptionist veered awkwardly from a dark open space behind a barely seen door to a large crafted reception desk. An eerie woman stood before them, her face unhealthy and the complexion of her skin was deathly.

Her almost transparent sky blue eyes stared cautioning, straining to deliver a message unspoken. 'You have landed in a house of prevailing monsters' I could comprehend from the gaze in her eyes.

"Mr and Mrs Brooklyn, I suppose," she finally let out her coarse voice.

"Indeed," replied Mr Harvey, smiling at the grim face staring back.

"We have been expecting you, room 360," she responded, handing over a single key. 'We' she had said in an empty hotel with none but her alone, how could there be a possibility of 'we'? There only was a dim red light focused on the two guests creating shadowed paths and blackening the unseen surrounding as if walking on a lit path towards an isolated faint grey door, and in they went to precede their love dynasty.

"Quite eerie, don't you agree?" Mrs Brooklyn finally suggested unleashing the traffic of thoughts in her head. In a profound manner showing concern in the choice of place. "Silent as a grave, no sign of inhibitors. Eerie indeed," she added. It was not in Mr Harvey's calendar to waste about time thinking of such in that precious moment. Fear not was all he had to say, quickly withdrawing from the subject and aroused the erotic waves. A soft, cool breeze rushed from the half-open window in the room, hollow, nothing more behind it. Even from the grim darkness of the hotel and out, the couple rose beautifully to the occasion suppressing intimacy of being in love. Intertwined to each other as hours passed. As gathering darkness beyond the lights of the window watched presenting itself as an invisible, unseen shadow, present yet hidden.

Behind the ridged wall, the psych pomp stood shrouded in a long, dark, black hooded cloak wielding a scythe. It was unusual, not seen frequently before. Alas, if I were to speak in haste, I would comment the destroyer came in that solitary room of the young birds watching the steady flame of a lamp Mr Harvey lit earlier. In that deep compassion where the two adjourned to rest on their gracing bed, true it is to say that any man could envy them drowned deeper into the essence of solid love with a bit of evident danger scathing in their midst. An unideal sense of touch.

He stood frozen and motionless like a scarecrow keenly studying Mr and Mrs Brooklyn. The sight was unexplainable in comparison to a mortal being. A black hollow revealed beyond his hood, beneath the sleeves of his cloak were as equally dark, no hand, no head, just a long hooded cloak hanging mid-air. Yet entirely visible he was portrayed beyond the night darkness with the silver shining of his scythe. It could be foretold that the air around him was cold as frost, damp and suffocating, maybe no air at all like the vast space. How I could describe death. The light from the glowing lantern did not showcase his creeping shadow as it would for a being and any solid object. The light vanished into the black entity. An eerie, invisible kind of man.

Every night the stranger approached, unnoticed, to the same spot half exposed, half hidden by the wall. "Dear husband," at one time Mrs Brooklyn uttered again.

"Yes, dear wife?" he responded, following to where she stood before the burning lantern.

"For three days now this lantern has been firm. I'm curious; has the oil not been consumed yet?" she went ahead to speak her conscious, she was quite a keen and observant lady. That was interestingly admirable to Mr Brooklyn, the reason why he grew fond of her. Nothing to Mrs Brooklyn should go unexplained not even the mere hooting of owls.

"Absolutely right you are. I did try putting it off but all in vain, sure there must be a mystery to this," he said as his wife commented once more, "Strange, strange indeed."

Harvey was convinced to address the issue the next morning. Fear was no longer the term to use in midnight dreary as a change of events smuggled dreadfully in The Grim Hotel.

It was not to the couple's anticipation of the sudden voices in the hotel. Not the ordinary sounds of casual conversations or pleasant laughter from incoming visitors. Nothing of the sort in particular, but instead a tone of endurable wrong. First was heard subdued shrillness then a tremendous bark of laughter echoed from a distance of supreme madness of the carnival season. It was unpleasing to both Mr and Mrs Brooklyn who chose to ignore after an abrupt merge of silence. "Still in for it?" Harvey asked, breaking the tension in the room.

"At all no second thoughts," she smiled, allowing her husband to take the lead. The intense pleasure from Harvey stirred up Mrs Brooklyn making her softly moan, embracing the body of her beloved steadily and gently. She delighted in the sensation of being wrapped in his arms. It wasn't yet enough, she signalled to her partner tightly clenching to his broad back, surrendering to his masculine energy. Indeed the threat still persisted, watching them, reading them and intruding their privacy, horridly portraying only one sign of his intentions, the burning lamp.

Hardly dawn reality of the world affected Harvey like visions. His eyes suddenly flashed with a fierce light awakened by a succession of loud and shrill screams. Mrs Brooklyn lay sound asleep to his thought. "Mary nay, did you hear that?" he whispered but no answer. He concluded to ask again, perhaps she never heard him. This time more audibly, "Did you not hear that?" While he spoke thus, some minutes elapsed without an answer. Petrified, Mr Harvey shook his wife's shoulder, his heart pounding in his chest but nothing. Complete stillness. Touch had no influence, totally unaltered. A terror intolerant to Harvey's blood as he shrieked back from the bed. Getting back to his senses, he moved to where she lay as the fragrance of decay wafted over his nose. Her skin generally assessed a cadaverous hue, eyes were naturally closed and limbs rigid at full length, her extremities were of icy coldness, her breathing was no longer apparent. Mrs Brooklyn lay there supervened by grim death.

Ghastly extremes of agony pervaded, an attack of extreme character that left Mr Harvey in a foul desolate condition, his life being rooted on his beloved wife. Knowing she was gone by the sight of her corpse pallid and placid, eyes lustless and lifeless. Grim darkness suppressed the earth, as Mr Harvey not entirely weak possessed a killing rage. He knew himself no longer; the fury of a demon possessed him.

The bitter remorse in his heart jeopardised his mortal soul and, in a plasmatic gust of violence, destroyed anything near him. A chair flung in the air breaking the windows in shatters, he turned the table upside down and seized a heavy club swinging it through overlying utensils. Thus was violence until he resigned to despair only to notice the still standing lantern eventually went off at the sudden demise of his wife.

For half an hour, Mr Harvey drained and whined at the deed. "Could I have pressed too hard? Was she suffering from a silent illness?" he asked himself these questions, unable to find an answer. He adopted ordinary means of relief and gradually pulled himself up as man should and lifted his wife's body, silently whisking out of the hotel into the cooling effect of the forest. The resemblance was quite unique between the outside and inside of Harvey's soul, cold as frost. Below the ghastly trees stands an inverted image of the trees, he performed a funeral procession and buried his late wife beneath the ghostly consecrated earth. "Long you shall dwell in my heart," he said, drawing away in insufferable gloom. Her memory would always be a shadow on his path. After his task drew to a close, he headed back into the hotel. The mystic psych pomp had followed standing before the grave like a tombstone, his decoration haunting her simple grave.

Harvey seized at the Gothic archway of the entrance hall with an utter depression of the soul, in the thorns of his bitter life. The bleak walls, vacant eye-like long windows and black oaken floor added to his confusion. The silence inside was indeed unbearable, not even a trace of the strange receptionist. Despicable, foul, excruciating, the tree of thoughts engulfed his mind. Peace came not to his aid but instead a vaporised distress. He dashed off to his room and slam shut the door violently, after which he sat down below it and buried his face in both his hands. He once again wept, struggling to reason off the nervousness that rendered over him.

How he despaired to find a remedy. The howls of a dark day stay in the Grim Hotel. Finally, he lifted his blue eyes streaming with the transparency of his tears. Behold what he saw, a dark fantasy, paranormal. It sure must have been a strange fantasy growing in Mr Harvey's mind. "Oh dear, this cannot be," he whispered feebly yet audibly as he stared in the eyes of a scrutinising observer. Strikingly similar with the diseased. Tremor pervaded Harvey's fray as the feminine voice uttered to whom she spoke to.

"The burning lantern is glowing no more, love," her voice a speaking guitar.

"Goodness, Mary nay, you are dead!" Mr Harvey rose to his feet and kept distance.

It was a dreading event of the future in his least expectation. She let out a lingering smile on her lips and mockery blush on her face. Her white floral nightgown fitted beautifully on her slim body reaching her upper thigh. Her skin was flawless, more beautiful than ever and her bronze, silky hair floated rather than fall upon her head. Harvey lapsed into insensibility no longer to be comprehended to what he had been subjected. His mouth remained widely extended in abounded astonishment to witness her alive.

The scenario was enough to scare somebody out of his wits. He blinked several times endeavouring to believe that much of what he felt and more so was due to the bewildered influence of the gloomy furniture of the room, of the dull wall and tattered belongings. As much as he would assume that, it was false, Mary nay was absolutely standing there.

"A premature burial, husband. Dead I am not," she sounded, her hair finally settled and appearance normal. What else can I say, was Harvey more astonished or excited? With less utterance, he wrapped his arms around his solid wife, distinctly feeling her warmth just as he used to. *But how*, he still thought. Isn't that he whisked out of a fantastic dream? "I do understand what you are feeling, husband," she spoke, able to read her husband's mind.

It could be that the hotel was creating some paranoid delusion in their heads, of a death that was never real, of grieving horror, of a sickening malevolence natured, thrilling every fibre in Harvey's body. Yes, indeed, it was. Not only did Mr Brooklyn experience this fantasy but also Mrs Brooklyn. Tears rushed out Mrs Brooklyn's eyes as they sat on the bed. She spoke, dictating, "If I well remember, at the hit of the midnight clock, still like a rock I saw you dead on this very bed. The lamp unlit and grotesque sounds arose like a disease growing upon me, I harkened but in vain. Outside in the biting wind, I laid you promiscuously in the solid granite weeping in heaving pain for my fallen husband. I was sure to have witnessed an imaginary strange being nearby but uncertain. Deplore of losing you was enough, thus I left the ground."

Mr Brooklyn was keen to listen, a surprisingly similar story. She continued, "You became a thought of shadows in my path that I returned to view your body once more only to find nothing. You vanished in the thin air like vapour. I knew where to look and waited until you approached with a similar thawed heart."

"Let us leave, Mary nay, not again shall I lose you to the deathly realm of this house," Harvey convinced his wife.

"Indeed, husband, let us leave, not even I will lose you to the deathly realm of this house." The new moon was now setting over the dawn, a portrait of approaching sunrise as the two newlyweds departed from The Grim Hotel. The psychpomp stood back at the hotel gates watching them slowly disappearing in the dense trees and finally gone.

Chapter 3
Behind the Red Door
'Struggles of a Psychotic Mind'

For who can wonder than man should feel a vague belief in tales of disembodied spirits wandering through those places which they once dearly affected, when he himself, scarcely less separated from his old world than they, is forever lingering upon past emotions and bygone times, and hovering, the ghost of his former self, about the places and people that warmed his heart of old?
—*Charles Dickens*

All evil seized control of my mind unleashing those monstrosities lurking behind the red door. To all extremities, I battled, suffered in a heaving excruciating pain to amend the broken. Yet the more I did vanquish the humanity and breed the wrath of inhumanity, my virtue slumbered; my evil kept awake by ambition; was alert and swift. Before the partial change noble was I like snow-white, sweet, and friendly, from a lineage of family regarded and preserved especially by all townsmen. Well, once upon a time I can say so, 1002 AD lived a family, was a fair tale of love, sisterhood and brotherhood. Our parents passionately bound by virtues yet about the midst other factors remained hidden from our souls.

Father saw soon his fate, found dead by his office door. Yet the quest for the truth retained silent rather impossible to explain. Not long Mother followed suit, then my siblings a year later. Before the demise, I failed not to hear the abrupt change of character, aggressive, abstruse and violent. Of eyes that spoke torture and death. The cover-up was suicide to those who believed not in magic, something of the sort. I so was fated to die similar yet reason came not on me to engage in so for this thought was monstrous to the soul, a purge of unseen wickedness. Truly was I a believer of the good, believer of a saviour, of redemption and eternal life.

To be said those monstrosities dwelled no further between the out worlds, earth. An established ritualistic format of the mind, generated from strong emotions. Beliefs that fuel the reminder for the effect desire. A torturous psychosis. Not long was the mark drew upon me, a deadly portal I hath thrown.

The offence declared grave among us. My brain reeled as I harkened, entranced to a melody more than ordinary as if endured with a serpent vitality. My conscious seized to be a friend, traded for a new one, brutal and weak. It was as if a disease drew upon me with hallucinations of the horror. The world I saw before me seemed not less than monsters, not even he I loved. I recall battling the good alongside my torments until I ended up no later in chains.

The religious called me possessed, did what they could to save me yet by the moments, I bewildered to pain and weakness. At times, I laughed, cried, tore and bled. Never the less did the horror clinging to my humanity let free my true self, normal for the while like a chance to bid farewell those whom I loved, before the complete consumption of my spirit.

Perhaps the aftermath of my isolated closure drew fancies upon me. As I mused silently in a chilly dark, massy, and grey dungeon, my case resulted to place me. At the corners were growing moulds and cobwebs decorating the cracking pallid walls, rodents squeak and scurry about. Most certainly, the air was damp and mildly foul, a loathsome plague spot to writhe.

I suddenly paused with an incredible blankness of my face. Blood crawled from within that blurred my sight to a wakening of delusions. My spirit inside frightened, terrified by this dark thing that sleeps beneath my flesh. And so the apocalypse unleashed of the unreal I presumed to see that can be described as grinding in the bones, a horror of the spirit that which cannot be exceeded at the hour of birth and death.

The memories recalled as I stood at the door of my father's office. He was normal, nothing of the odd. The room, however, remained questionable, papers spread about aimlessly spilt ink from inkpots and blotters like an effect of an earthquake. Yet did his face portray no anger, nothing more only the ordinary. I watched him mumble in whispers conversing with himself. He rose from the sit, his eyes widening with a grotesque hue of the pupil till the whispers grew louder by each word uttered.

The resolution embarked fright upon me forced to watch an awakening madness sickening to the heart. I could incline there dwelled a second presence in the room, invisible and deathly as I witnessed the terror in my father's lips as he now yelled and sweating feverishly. In an instant was evoked a tremendous fit of rage spitting words to the unseen. "Come no closer, leave me be darkness! Depart from me torment!" he repeated these words again and again. He tumbled over the office furniture controlled by anguish. Everything tangible he grasped went flying about the room in an attempt to bruise that what he presumed to be haunting him.

In the midst, Mother walked in past me into the room. Had she not seen me by the door? *Quite impossible*, thought I. Truly my nerves pondered meaning I must have had a solid body to respond to the trammels of horror crouching before me. "Mother!" the words flew out of my mouth in motives to seek attention, some show of concern witnessing such. Was I only but a child succumbing to this terror yet nothing, in complete vain. The situation tenfold more wicked at the abrupt thought of death. Dead, am I? When? For what cause? Certainly if so, it must have been quick to feel the rip.

"Keep your calm, husband, none other but I is alongside you," my mother spoke gently, holding up her husband to her chest with care. Indeed, she loved the English subject yet tears strolled down her cheeks, cold and salty that seemed to burn around her sad eyes the more they poured. Sore I could describe her too, feel like she had faced this more than once, and by each occurrence, she faded all hope. But my father's eyes bore no soul by now, a dark void corrupt in his mind and heart for this time he drew her to be the serpent. "Leave me be, demon! Perish!" The insanity, she saw it too. The scathing demon that tormented her beloved, and she began to sing feebly yet audibly.

Sweet is your love
Bitter is your pain
O' dearly beloved
We suffer both the same way
My heart is not in better dismay
For I too am pale and grey.

Soon shall be your sound no more
For your spirit is by the door
Slow and steady your breath at its pause
So you may rest once and for all.

Finally silenced and broke into sobs staring at the body feeble and in pain. Most certainly, Mother knew the time like childbirth waited a few more seconds as her husband wearied off till eventually, he was no more. His life and torment finally ended. The shocking disbelief I was subjected to left me into a breathless paralytic pause. Had this become so hideous that I dashed off to my father's corpse panting and weeping heavily. Those eyes with no lustre and pallid like I viewed at his funeral. By then Mother was no longer in sight, she vanished only her shadow trailing along the long dark corridors into their chamber. I dared follow but she was swift like a ghost. Nor did I have the motive of questioning her cause to end her beloved's life for I saw clearly her grief.

Death was only mercy though indefinite to where one's spirit proceeds from the body. And so did Mother resolve to the same. She was there caressing the bedside to where father laid, and I called once then twice, "Mother, speak to me please." But once more no response, just sobs. It was silent yet the weeping was screaming to my ears creating some pain and discomfort, somewhat a paranormal kind of cry. Gradually, her head turned to my angle, her gaze that of a mother to her child for I yearned the magnificence of love. Indeed, I spotted it once more since her demise. Thus, her voice suppressed the atmosphere, words of caution and uncertainty, "It's coming for you too. To all of us, oh the darkness."

Fear drew me to stagger back, my heart pounding off my chest. Mother vanished for the second time in the blink of an eye this time surely perished from the fancies. The dark veins now crawled more beneath my eyes as I witnessed the impossible. A bizarre I failed to familiarise even with keenness. A woman rather old and grim. The darkness. "The authentic darkness of my pervaded fray!" I muttered.

"Yet is, my dear, to see its totality," she responded back, the sharp cast of those eyes reviving a grotesque force upon me. The pressure was pressing to the point of embedding pain for I could feel my spirit ripping out of the flesh. Most certainly, I yelled with all effort to escape the crouching evil, and I fought back grim figures surrounding me like tombstones.

For a moment, I seized fighting my inner demons, we were on the same side now. The blurriness faded and my vision resumed to the ordinary. Too late, I must say for I braced and delighted it like wine. My rebirth to the unholy was still no occasion for joy, ambushed like a blood-drawn carnival. Had I become a portent of evil to the environment circulating around my den? They watched in pity as my rage struggled to force out of the dungeon and rip each soul parading before me. "You monsters, how I loathe you, all of you!" the unreal voice barked to the innocent gathering crowd, and I fell into a deep seizure of this extreme psychosis.

No later was I sedated with shock therapy to induce the seizure. So must have been thought to cure, perhaps the monster would seize to be vicious. Yet was I succumbed to perfect oppression for the fear awoke the more, stimulated to wreak havoc within me. For how could such be overcome, that chocking smell of plagues, echoes of dismay of no empathy, no sense of life but dreaded existence of the unfriendly. Had I lain afterwards in my thin bed, complete with illness till once the oppression failed to proceed.

Yet again, I saw her, now younger, still pallid beyond the black shadowy cloak she wore. Among the crowd of humans, the phantom stood closer and glances deeper. "You, the darkness, leave me be," said I feebly yet audibly. The crowd gazed once more in sounds mutters, "She is speaking to whom now?" Clearly, the shadows of horror could be seen by none but me.

For the moment, I failed to feel this physical pain that burnt like a blue ritual flame. I watched into the depths of her dark spirit but her watch to mine was no dark and cruel. It was pitiful and broken, to which I could clearly, for the first time, see the story behind her rage. Of course, her mortal side indeed fell in love with my father. He broke her heart yes, for he loved her not the same. "The smell of my heaving has drawn you to at last withdraw my soul from the body, so get on with it," said I with complete conviction to end this gloom for life bore no meaning. The silence broke when her voice uttered young and softly like an inner voice ringing in my mind words of forgiveness and freedom.

So certain was I to assume the end of me, the last light, the flashing memories of my life, opt of my future fated not to pass. The reality eventually became clear that I was spared from death. Never had I felt entirely at ease, normal again as I panted away the fatigue of a horrid race. I turned to ask but she was gone, no longer in the midst of this solitude. Even to my conscious, she departed never to be known again yet I wished she was not in haste. Many questions had I wanted to ask of her. But certainly, it gave her no peace either. For the better part, I had a second chance to live once more, free from a psychotic fathom pursuing my being, to embrace the sunlight and watch the gardens and hiding meadows.

Chapter 4
Teles
'Tragic Love Story'

Love is not a consequence. Love is not a choice.
Love is a thirst. A need as vital to the soul as water is to the body.

—*Colleen Houck*

So can be said, confidently assumed from the unhidden expression of one's face that he was deeply in love. Christopher King. Just a young sailor with many ambitions and dreams like seeking adventure in many seas across the world. Certainly not for any profitable reason but only view closer a new land, in every one of that he encountered, he failed not to put it to writing each bearing its own uniquely distinct name from his thoughts, a library of many imaginations. Indeed, I have mentioned earlier Christopher fell in a trance for a woman, a rare one not of his race or genus. Teles.

Many spectral images drew inside my mind his lustful desires that lead first his fate. Certainly not do I portray him as fond of maenads (women) for he was noble yet intimately obsessed to that he found irresistibly stunning to his sight. Fascinating, something of the sort. As I wrote Christopher's story, in every memory I recollected my emotions bewildered my fray and the knowledge I presumed to have could flicker like a burning candle, fade and finally vanish like a desert mirage. So felt like writing a letter to an already departed soul. Nothing more but a mere decoration crafted by one's own hand and the scroll fitted into a wine bottle.

I agree not that young Christopher was in love, to my conclusion it was an irresistible sire he failed to repel. In one morning glad, I bid the lad farewell as he set sail into the sea. There it was enthusiasm to land somewhere new, the remarkable determination to explore all edges of the earth and later return to dictate the story. At that point, I was expecting so, till the news came in a scroll delivered to the intended by a homing pigeon. The young sailor and his crew journeyed west of Naples at midday in a windless calm, at an incredibly beautiful yet rocky island surrounded by cliffs. The most fascinating so it was believed to be, magnificent regarded by they who have set eyes upon it. Most I hear have never returned. The 'flowery' island, Anthemoessa also referred by others as Sirenum scopuli.

That, if I am indeed correct, was the dwelling place of Christopher's heart, Teles, the bearer of all he possessed, heart, mind, body, and soul. As he sailed across the sea, making melodious chats with his crew and feeling the ocean waves tossing about the waters. They sang, danced, drunk and laughed. ***"Mai, mai multe triumph la comorile purtat in mare,"*** *(More, more jubilation at the treasures within the sea).* He could chant, consumed every bit by his voyage, deepened into the sparkles of adventure and fantasies. The image suddenly drew upon the mariners, picturesque and mythical to the eyes. Too much of a delusion to be conceived by the planet earth, Anthemoessa.

Sweet music perforated the cold mystic air of the island sinking impetuously with the tides of gentle emotions. Rhythmic waves from a harp sliding past one another systematically creating illusions of control that vanquished many. This and more arrested their attention from which a voice arose beautifully in suppressed tones. Indeed, it was uniquely exquisite to the ears of men. Christopher had listened to his beloved, a daughter of the sea god Phorcys wooing him to surrender before her.

**Mai aproape-eugen mea dragos musca din mere
Mea atrăgătoare inima mea declara tu numai
tu.
Simți bate pieptul meu rapid resipraţie in
Plămănii mei se apropie de dragostea mea lung
au fost de așteptare pentru tine.**
"Teles, Oh! Mea iubită aramă am tănji pentru tine."

(Teles Oh! My brazen lass, I yearn for you) said he countless times in a possessed sensation. For he and many of them became enchanted to certainty, absolute compulsion luring the blood in their veins, the flesh of their bodies and the soul of their mortality. Truly and completely bewildered. Soon the ship led them to wherever it did with the blowing direction of the wind unaided. Oh! I could foresee the tragedy, the forerunner of death and corruption attempting to do her deed. Her singing lyre led the trees, led the wild beasts of the wilderness, and led the heart that which longed for her.

Pardon me, for this story saddens me so. A little while to compose myself once more. My hand fails to write at ease, oh! The horror I presume to have been after. But his story had to be made known though I wished for the impossible that he would stand before me this instant. The childhood memories we did share together bound by a common assignment to venture the world like *'Sinbad And The Seven Seas'*, the only barrier at the time was I to have fallen ill that I failed to tag along. I keep my vow so let's proceed.

Nearer and nearer the distance did grow, the ship crashing into the island against the jagged cliff. Still, the lure pervaded relentlessly taking with it mortal lives. I meant to say many died at the fall of the ship with less pain or maybe none at all. Their conscience completely drawn from them far before the tragedy, no voice, no struggle like a passing plague of pestilence.

And of Christopher, what of him? Did he die with the crowd? And so I thought, what else could be the possibility. That he darted off in an errant? Or we presume he found life from the fancies? I think not. I received the scroll that he survived not. I read the letter with more than one eye, with more brains to contemplate the words. Those words that indeed broke my heart. I must confess I desired him deeply, as he loved the special sea nymph so did I love him. I knew him more than she did, grew up by his side yet he saw me not more than a sister.

But eventually, the love, like his life, crumbled to dust. Of course, he survived the shipwreck for the while just to set eyes upon her who sang irresistibly sweetly no less sad. It lapped both body and soul in a fatal lethargy yet he did not mind.

Mai aproape-eugen mea dragos musca din mere
Mea atrăgătoare inima mea declara tu numai
tu.
Simți bate pieptul meu rapid resiprației
Plămănii mei se apropie de dragostea mea lung
au fost de așteptare pentru tine.

The song persisted now more closely and audibly, graceful, compelling, earthly, transcending, and powerful. Alas! Christopher King saw Teles, a muse of the lower world, a siren. His eyes widened with amazement as he wandered through the wild solitudes of fantasy. *"Remarcabil, frumos este ea vedea făta mea. Oh! Teles,"* (Remarkable, beautiful is she I view before me. Oh! Teles) said he in a low tone, clearly speaking to himself.

The untamed creature portrayed a precious trace of beauty, her skin perfectly clear and compelling with no scarcely seen acne. From the sweetest recesses of her lovely, long bridal locks, one would be eager to ask how she could manage to capture the scent of a summer's day in the traces of her hair. Intertwined with soft waves and a pretty floral crown. Vanilla perfumed, yellow buttercup, white daisy, purple violet and ruby red asphodels.

Teles, she was indeed exquisite to capture a wayward traveller like Christopher King in her habitat of many-coloured grass, Anthemoessa. Ay, look further into the curve of her body, brazenly exposed, burgeoning and creamy breasts. Her waist and below resembled the body of a bird feathered and scaly feet. He failed not to notice large wings penetrating from her back. Christopher condemned staying on the island with the spectral figure lolling there in her meadow. Round her were heaps of corpses rotting away, rags of skin shrivelling on their bones.

Should I go on to the end of this draft? Must I subject myself into this self-torture I cannot retreat? I kissed him once to pass forth a cue. Certainly not should I have done so. It was fate we were not meant to be. Besides, he lusted to taste another's lips soft and red as roses, eyes blue as lavender. He had seen what her kind do. They hunt, they kill, they dispose of. What they are cannot love, cannot care and pity as I can love him. They are cursed and chained to grandiose evils that damn humans to their fate. Christopher desired to lust her despite. Could I have warned him of this? But none could have seen it coming, if only I knew so earlier.

The trammels of confusions did not end there. The siren glanced with friendly eyes that arrested a man's focus. She blushed and bowed with her luxuriant tresses, in disdain and unseen inhumanity half buried in alien hair. Her intentions were absolutely foul, nothing of the good. The young lad, my beloved pal was trapped whatsoever. No gap to slip, well, not as much as a bridle's breathe. How Christopher fancied that Teles was coming to embrace him, how he loathed they who saw her as a demon in disguise. Besides, he had seen it in her eyes she bore no ill will only that Teles was different, unlike other maenads, unlike I to his assumption.

Truly if she consumed the pile of mortal bodies that surrounded her like barrier reefs, what made Christopher so special? Nothing. Not even the handsomeness of his face or the hazel colour of his eyes. Not even if he was a god. Surely, what hope is there for him? His heart bits strong indeed for someone in such danger.

My hands are getting weary at the verge of writing this sad story. No more booze is left among the shelves of this hollowed hall to give me false aspirations. "*Aah!* Curses!" I wish not to have been the author of this, but only because I loved him that I engaged in doing so. My readers could fall in undeniable suspense if I so fail to continue, what choice do I have. Let all of them know that I fell in love with he who threw it like chaff in the vast air for a sea nymph. If so happened to you, what would you have done? Well, I can withhold the terror, the reason you can read to this end, the reason I shall not seize till complete in every aspect of that I recall.

And so he believed that Teles was coming forth to kiss him. Anyone in sight would have thought she was. But the truth remained that she did not at all kiss him but fed on his flesh and blood. Perhaps he let her cut through his flesh with her carnassial, watching and sniffing at the entrails of his own blood. The wretched untamed beast that Teles truly was. The inhabitants of Anthemoessa could not adhere to this relationship between species; one had a soul the other failed to have one.

Forever lost was he with an incredulous blankness of his face, the relaxed tissues in his body, a breath in his lungs not cherished for it was his last. For a moment, he breathed a delirious bliss then in a slow and steady way turned from the weary of the world, the final beam of light he viewed from the midday sun fluctuating before they slam shut then darkness, nothing more. His blood and body remained in the island among the pile of mortal corpses. She caressed his corpse, pale as moonlight's veil but in the next moment, Christopher's memory faded.

Teles resigned in search for a new wayward traveller as she opened up her large wings and fled, away from my late friend's decay. Her plight to always and forever be alone was discrete; there is no name for it just the sincere facts. Teles' song brewed Anthemoessa in every way to appease her feed, until one could be brave enough someday to pierce a bronze sword through her heart. Until then the devious conspired better, today than yesterday. Crying in rhythmic waves about the land and ocean's natural phenomena.

Shall I tell you a secret?
And if so I do will you get me
Out of this bird suit?
I don't enjoy it here
Squatting on this island
Looking picturesque and mythical.
With these two feathery maniacs
I do not enjoy singing
This trio fatal and valuable.
I shall tell the secret to you
To you, only to you
Veer closer. This song
Is a cry for help! Help me!
Only you, only you can
You are unique.

    I believe I have satisfied you indeed; no more can I proceed from this point. This has come to be the end of my pages. The last bottle of booze is left that I beg to depart and consume it the next in hopes of drowning in the ghost of Christopher King that has chosen to haunt me, appearing before me in tears and distaste. I fail not to feel his presence by day in complete anguish and torment that forbids him to push on into the afterlife. He whispers again and again in pain and lust, *"Te iubesc, Teles. (I love you, Teles.)"*

Chapter 5
Declarations of Love
'A Certain Dream'

One awakens refreshed from every nightmare.
—Marty Rubin

In a little sense of devious fear, we can indeed get lost in its destruction, act out of frustrations, and react with less amount of wit and aggression. Peace came not to my aid, comfort or joy. At that one night, I dreamt of my beloved Apithord. The losing fear that I wish to be redeemed, the nothingness I felt inside, frozen solemnly without rescue. In a matter of agony and deplore enough it seemed not. Instead, more I felt, particularly plucking out my only existing life in a dreadful midnight suicide. Sinister to one's self. Certain it was not, overwhelming it was neither. Enthusiastic I was to evoke my mission that daring night in the aim of escaping such darkness, such emptiness.

I had stayed locked in our hotel room, under lock and key I was certain. There was no trace of him to my wake as much as I opt to feel his masculine embrace, love and affection. It was an entirely lifeless room with the grey canvas walls that appeared pallid in the night reflection of the moon. On it was pinned the portrait of love, our love shared before an event of sudden vanish.

Apithord had disappeared in thin air. In the romantic air of an exquisite night, the first we ought to lie together on our gracing bed, on the soft cream sheets and puffy pillows. I could smell the fragrance from its fabric, lavender, I could tell. Certainly, this was not my anticipation of such irony. The illuminating moon rays lit part of the room and my skin, together with my white nylon nightgown that barely reached my knee that bore my appearance to that of a beautiful ghost.

With no sense of direction, I rose from the bed possessed by the crescent moon and night serenity. My spirit was sinking somewhere cold, desperate beyond steady wits. Anything was better than to be alone. Closer and closer I headed for the gazing window, I lifted it, a step I dared make in the outside cold. Not before long my whole body was hanging out, firmly balancing on the edges of the building outside. Like a bird's feathers, the erect hairs on my body caressed the wind's might. Take me wrong when I say that I pondered. Not at all did I. Not at all did even shudder to the effect of a winter breeze, of the biting wind and driving snow.

I stood there ridged only that my long, black, silky hair waved violently all over my head in some occasions blurring my vision. For what reason would I have to attempt such dreary in such haste? It was the nothingness I had become without Apithord, the first and last man my life remained rooted to. Love indeed it was. Like a poisonous apple, bite just once and the venom conjures every part of my living being. Like a portion of addictive wine, a taste of it, the heart, mind and body bow down to its adoration.

And so the more I thought the more boldness I gained to jump off the edge in an instant. Nothing had I felt so intolerant to the blood until then. In most situations, on many occasions, they say that the passage of time would heal all wounds. But the greater the loss, the deeper the cut. The more difficult the process to become whole again. Yet in all that, all I needed to hear was his voice calling out my name and save from the dark, I perused to render myself.

Before I succumbed to the unforgiving act leading me into my grave, my ears were suddenly altered by the sound of a singing violin at a near yet far distance. The music was familiar to the sweet melody streaming into my earlobe. This rhythm was played by only one heart, one kind. Apithord. The musical tone wafted from up the hotel building. Fear came not on me as I walked my way along the edges drowned by the sweet music of a heart. None in the building seemed to notice a suicidal lady passing across their windows outside.

On the approach of the first window sat an old woman inside, seemingly lonely in an open vacuum. Dead she looked yet dead she was not. She had laid an old man's portrait on her thighs hardly looking at it. From that expression, I could tell that she was paralysed in thoughts lost in her head. Nothing at all would alter her movement. On to the next window, I witnessed a mask party, clown face masks painted in black tears. One could not justify the expression of their faces not seen, glad or gloomy. I went further, climbing up tangible parts of the tall wall of the hotel flaring with the midnight energy. I was like a dwelling night ghost endeavouring about unnoticed. No one was concerned about a love tragedy. That which kept me clinging unafraid of losing balance. His sweet melody could not leave me free, driving in me a life to spare. I finally arrived at the window to which the music penetrated. Indeed, to my expectation, it was him, deepened by his play in a solitary room with a lit lamp beside him. Not at all did I wish to destruct him but instead listen further as he did it.

With such passion that I envied, commitment and love just like that I had for him. Lucky, I must confess I was to be in possession of such a man whom I feared had vanished yet wrong I was. There he was in front of me separated by the window glass. He turned to face me anguished by what I was doing, and he seized with a mad rushing to the window. We stared for a moment both our palms touching the same spot of the glass as if we were really touching. With it, I could see a revelation of unending love, the awaited desire. "I love thee," I whispered, my warm breath blurring the transparent glass. It felt like I had been sleeping for a thousand years and now to open my eyes to everything.

Immediately, he lifted up the window and I lost balance tipping off from the edge. But just in time for him to catch my arm. Fear and ambush drew in his liquid green eyes. I could see him more clearly, terrified and tears dropping. Afraid he was to lose me just as I was to lose him. Apithord loved me, holding on tight with an effort to pull me up as I floated in the open air. I struggled to pull up but in vain. Was it now too late? That both of us would lose each other forever. One by death, another by loss. Despite the adoring effort, the gravity fighting against me was weighing me down into the empty dark hole underneath. By that, I meant the ground was too far below, visible only as a dark entity.

I felt his heart ponder, the attempt to rescue me before I came undone, before my blood would seize to run. Unfortunately, without talk, without a voice, without a soul, I slipped off his fingers. My eyes shut as I dived into the grim atmosphere. I surrendered to death chanting the words, "I love thee, beloved." I could feel parts of my spirit tearing away in bits before I could completely hit the ground to my last breath.

Before that horror, a flash of light swept across my eyes, and they were forced open. I could physically feel a sense of warmth and comfort enveloping my body. I blinked once then twice making effort to fully wake up and there he was. Apithord was holding me to his chest between his arms; his eyes naturally shut forming a beautiful curve. I felt the steady breathing and beating in his chest. It felt relieving, especially from the dreadful dream. Not with an intention of ruining the moment, I laid back. And so we stayed under the umbrella of each other's love till dawn.

Chapter 6
The Author's Authentic Disease
'A Strange Edge of an Author'

Look on the grave where thou must sleep
Thy last, and strongest foe;
It is endurance not to weep
If that repose seem woe.

—*Emily Brontë*

Life, as described in my self-written journal, is not precisely through the all desire of men a clear, direct assumption of only fortune, of all beauty and luck. For few so might be the case, for others not exactly or to some the total opposite. At certain events, a state can change to be defined as harsh and unfavourable that we tend to despair and condemn ourselves to innumerable shadows of gloom. Poverty, broken affairs, epic failures and illnesses, the basis of my suffering. The rotten erect of unsavoury existence, madness, so hideous and intolerable fantasts only that it remains facts of the reality, the unsmiling dourness to vulgar garrulity, so sick unto death with that long agony endeavouring to the extremities.

These of my true facts were pitied, the catalogue of human misery that naturally leads more than hundreds to anticipate the epic downfall of a prominent and spectacularly authentic author. The sad means to which my works globally enthralled assumed to have come to rest alongside the figure to which people assumed to one possibly might have played a part of death in a pageant, by the distorted wellness. The state at which I laid upon my bed strangely adapted to the scenario that hope can be said to be lost, to which one can air out calculations of the time of death. Doctors regarded as the most intelligent and highly experienced in this field of study apprehended to have never encountered such disease with that character of an epic termination and fatality.

Rigorous experiments were the conclusion of my state not positive to fancy a second chance of earthly existence. The degree of this pestilent momentum released intoxicating pheromones in the air around me, hues of the contagious cues of the disease, of methylated spirits and alcohol, rotted away bandages, and pungent medical odours.

The image for one to see me in such fatal paralysis, vitally distinguished from others as hideous and grotesque would certainly writhe into dire incomprehensible nightmares, delusions of a typically psychotic man. It was now more than three weeks after my supposedly dead portrait yet fully alive was I, terribly frightening. Completely no comprehendible indications to suggest so or otherwise unlike a month ago when traces of life would still be of visible notice in its delirious form. The struggle and suffering to keep alive, the raging thirst, the severe chest pains, the anticipated influx of the woundedness, the migraines and the delirium.

Now at this particular period, I resulted to remain senseless and externally emotionless. My face wore a pale and placid leaden hue like frosted flesh with lingers of slight colour around the cheek region and in some joints like the knuckles of my hands and feet, elbows, and knees. My thin lips were blue and seemingly sewed with numerous cracks. The only preventative of premature burial was the warmth remaining in the mild notice and upon application of the mirror to the lips, it would be detected a torpid, unequal, and vacillating reaction of the lungs. Emaciation of the body was extreme that the skin appeared sucked in by the bones to a jigsaw fit. My eye sockets became horrifically sunken forming a black, depressed void. Perspiration burst out from the pores, clamping like tiny drops of mercury upon my forehead. The extreme fatigue and general weakness induced me to remain unnaturally prostrate and intolerably still countenance.

S. Pavlov my current physician in attendance was very keen and curious about this event that he had never witnessed before in either of his patients in his entire life. He had gone through most of my profiles in search of families or close relatives here in France I must have heard close by or even in the distance to prepare my burial. Sadly, I heard none, brought up in an orphanage for the most part of my life and later left to strife to make a living. It was agonising for the man to handle this case, furthermore made to keep watch of this bizarre condition that made no sense. My lips made no motive to move as to utter a word, just but an open door for respiration.

In one midnight dreary, not so long after my regular checkups by my physician, a very unusual occurrence happened that could gravely alter the spirit to shudder. But at this point, the response did not necessarily mean my disturbing condition was in a better state of recovery. Neither of what I experienced in the first stages of my illness. The state of this matter was only seen during sleepwalking. Suddenly, all my power was exerted to the eye muscles, and I flipped them wide open and paused at that without blinking for the rest of the time. In a short while, my lips loosened, and I was able to speak though with difficulty.

I let out a groan that alerted the nurse hired to keep watch of me. He had exhaustedly slumbered on a chair beside the bed and was accompanied by the keeper who was also asleep. "Good Lord, Mr Mort, you are awake!" said the nurse and rushed to make a call to S. Pavlov who came almost immediately after the phone call.

God, was he fascinated, amazed or, to assume, shocked to for once observe the colour of my eyes that he had not seen for months since I elapsed into this cadaverous realm. "Please, get a glass of water for the patient," requested S. Pavlov to the keeper who rushed to get him water. His voice was that of kindness and pity as he tranquilly asked, "Would you like some water, you surely must be thirsty." I, on the other side, made no utterances, neither was I aware that S. Pavlov sat beside me or even spoke. Like a comatose patient unable to initiate voluntary actions. However, comatose patients exhibit complete absentee of wakefulness, senses and motion. I was in a perfect trance of something else so strange and uncomprehensive. S. Pavlov slightly lifted my pillow elongating my position to an obtuse angle and steadily poured the water down my throat.

I made another groan, this time more apparent, that made the physician even more pleased. He was not, however, satisfied with this and dared ask, "George Mort, do you recall me whatsoever?" What made S. Pavlov ask this was the expression of my sight that seemed not to be drawn to his attention. Feebly yet audibly, I spoke but not to his precise question.

"Yes, I heard, that voice a terror to my spirit." To his uncertain remarks, he asked again and again.

"Mr Mort, are you feeling any discomfort whatsoever?"

Yet again I spoke, "Let us make way to what holds me. Refrain from the exit to have me pass." S. Pavlov was getting convinced that I might be still in slumber.

He confirmed this by asking, "Are you still in your slumber?" The rate at which he perused me to speak aroused more than the answers he needed to hear to a much bizarre performance.

The rigidity of my limbs stabilised as for my hands to which I lifted steadily, though not too high up, and pointed at the door which was wide open since the arrival of the physician. "Wait upon me, I said wait," said I. I rose up shuddering as I did like someone under extreme starvation. My sight remained fixed towards the direction of the door, and this frightened the latter parading around me, they did not, however, interrupt. Their mouths were agape, oppressed, and totally induced into rapturous astonishment not at all to be sensible.

So was believed to be Somnambulism. A behaviour disorder originated during deep, prolonged periods of sleep that result in walking or performing other complex behaviours while in slumber. This occurred to me throughout the episode. However, there was logic to this theory presented by the physician that in my case could not be further elaborated, which provided a realistic idea of a possible cause of sleepwalking to be as a result of certain medication. The others include febrile illnesses, sleep deprivation and sedative agents (including alcohol) that wasn't my case. I steadily proceeded to the outer night as the physician and other followed. At this point, I stood gazing north at logically nothing. The silence outside had by now intervened with supremeness aside the distant hooting of owls and whistling of the crickets. The time was already past midnight.

I sat under a dry lifeless tree, its large penetrating branches spread outwards that appeared like a dark, deathly creature in the ebon blackness of the absolute night. I had nothing at all to fear for I was entirely not in my senses, meaning I held no direct conscious with my body. My spirit would have been concluded to be totally gone. I turned my head on both sides, left to right respectively as if clearly staring at two possible beings. For me, however, this I cannot deny having been no one at the event, most certainly there was but only to my vision. Another, I presumed, was up above my head. As to describe the staff, they somewhat were repulsively distorted to give an audience a feeling of extravagant and uncomfortable bizarreness.

The creation of such would be extremely licentious and absurd as a carelessly and possessively embellished painting. But now in the form of a human creation left undone with meshes of decayed flesh fixed to a perceptibly visible skeletal body, figures of firth and aspects of meth. Their colour though vividly visible in the dark, was dull and shaded as if the effect of an extraterrestrial atmosphere. To my hallucinations, they overspread and disfigured the tree darkening the immediate surrounding and profuse intoxicating pungent of rot.

It was within the view that everything became blackened, totally silenced to the mute. It had been like I stirred strange and frightening images. Was what I sought to dream this hideous? We know of nothing so agonising upon earth, dream or fantasize of anything so hideous in the realms of nethermost hell. None could grapple at the shadowy fancies that crawled upon me had they seen it. They could utmost insinuate me to be mad. The latter stood far back, but they could only note me, the patient who sat still under just but a ghastly tree stand.

I was chained by such superstitious impressions of intolerable horror. My fluctuating conscious resumed its position in my body. "Oh you leave me all the hopeless and affray, how long, how long till I waste?" I spoke feebly, my teeth chattering.

Now to the right, the other spoke, "You morn oh, tomorrow you shall renew but first upon your death bed you must lay." The exceeding death seemed not to halt at this point. The painful and oppressive illness that consumed me until I wished death suppressed. Oh, the pity felt by my physician who remained prostrate by the door anticipating what would happen next. I, on my side, lacked words to respond to this pursuit.

Once again, the feathery influence lifted my spirit and I felt, for a moment, lifeless and the other spirit thus evoked. "Yes, you do me good to visit me this day. Oh, yes, I have waited, waited long enough." It felt like a complete conflict between death and my spirit and my emaciated living corpse as the host. My conscious once more flashed to the surface of my existence.

"Return me into the earth; revive my state for I have many more stories to tell. Why still here? Why must you taunt me?" They were totally unmoved by my desolate condition, for what use was it to none who existed as a life form, none with no love nor hate. To be particular emotionless.

"The journey has thus begun; none who is gone can be recovered," the one above spoke, steadily sailing down in smoky hues. I pleaded more audibly though restricted,

"Please, thou reclaims me too soon. What of my books, my readers? Oh! The conjuring suspense."

"What of your sins that deprive you wake?" the one to my left muttered. Yet again, the other existence shuffled me off my mortal coil and reigned.

That was the last I felt my soul within me. Now it was gone and if not completely confined until the official announcement of my time of death. This condition was not altered for a quarter of an hour as the physician accompanied by the nurse and keeper watched my conversation with presumable nature. They could see nothing of the horrid phenomenon. Eventually, the state of the living corpse bid the figures farewell like a…statue. "Goodbye, goodbye…" repeatedly waving about the hand at nothing but the passing wind. "Goodbye! Goodbye…" Eventually, the living corpse stood and proceeded back into the shelter with no utterances towards S. Pavlov or any other with him at the event. Steadily laid back on the bed with an upwards position and remained deathly still like I had been before the supposed sleepwalking.

Now S. Pavlov veered closer to review my state. In this severe and long-continued illness, my breathing was now in slow and silent inhalation and exhalation as I assumed a cadaverous hue and the lingering colour on my cheek and joints had vanished. A horrid paleness and icy coldness suppressed and my general posture was in a relaxation mood. Eventually, my breathing seized, to be no longer apparent. And this was the simultaneous and irreversible onset of apnea and unconsciousness in the absence of all circulation, ready for the long improvised dirges.

Chapter 7
Shakespeare's Romeo and Juliet: The Sequel Fancies of Friar Laurence
'A Tale from a Once-Existing Love'

I had reasoned this out in my mind that one do I have liberty to and the other not do I. The liberty to end my life as it keeps me free from its repeated scowls. One I have no liberty to erase is pure love greatly endured at the period of its reign.
—*Faridah Otieno*

I presumed to have seen the last civil feud, the profound flow of blood, the bodes of my soliloquy, the love in Verona, the lovers' impassioned pledges, the dread sentence of death, the last distinct exaggeration. At times, a bizarre of exquisite guilt, of pain, of the massacre, gust calamities that in this accord appear long in the agony, the thirst, the sickening thoughts, and the delirium. I have most certainly seen the extent of this and many calamities before, foul confessions from men with souls of lead, wedded an asylum of lovers with a well authentic disease assumable to be of the mind. As this, my position of religious affluence has I seen not scarce Pepsis of legitimate fiction. My kind bears witness for not alone the holy mass and the white robes patches the insoluble and delirious fancies of the vital world.

In my saying of love, the purity of it undiluted only authentically the colour, the pheromone, and the exquisite hues of the urge lives more to the moment of death and perhaps beyond these extremities known not of aside the dead. As to why had I thought of such possibilities with uncertainties? Hate so shadowy and vague yet no golden bow irreparably broken for love so pure and keenly felt arise, claims to which I had never viewed until then. A lad from the house of Montague that looted away his boyhood on poesy, anticipated his youth in dreamy lethargies and his lass from the house of Capulet overwhelmed with beauty, pride and energy. The irony rather startling of two warring factions existing in droves on a world best for plundering.

I had mentioned earlier that I had never seen such till then. Romeo and Juliet's demise at that moment plunged me to a tumult of despairing cries. Their fresh, undecayed cadavers laid before the church to which I remained forced to look a hideous dizziness suppressing me. Their coffin though warmly and softly padded, provided with a lid fashioned upon the principles of the volt door with the addition of spring portrayed a peaceful rest yet sad unrest. No other species of wretchedness had ever birthed into being as to what association I took part to result to such foredoomed agony. As I recalled the portion meant not to harm but deceive death, I gave to her that which even the most rigorous medical tests would fail to establish any material distinction between the state of the patient and what we conceive of absolute death.

Upon my bed at that sickening hour of the night, though the slumber was usual, the weather to the peak of its foulness, in the heavens the stars inhibited in the dark cosmos not to be seen and atmosphere thick with salt, so unepic of it. As to assume this was an ordinary night like all others, nothing confoundedly amazing like the eve of Easter. The period of time that one to that accord of a sober eye of reason would question, the buffoons and improvisatory, the dancers and musicians, the beauty and wine, all of these appliances of pleasure summoned to celebrate the death of a prominent being in the lives of all. To that, after all, was also a celebration of an unusual magnificence, the resurrection. But this case was seen as mad. I consented to sleep only to rush into a world of fantasy, just but a moment of what felt like sleep paralysis.

Suddenly, there emerged a cool icy breeze unlike that of the night, from an origin far beyond that in Verona. A strange fragrance, not the strong peculiar odours of moist grass that matches the period, rather one to assume as an angelic gust sent from beyond another new existence. As I lay motionless with endeavours to recollect my senses to explain this vivid phantasm, an impatient, jeering voice called as if a spirit was speaking within. "Get thee up, I say wake, Father. How canst thou tranquilly sleep?" it persisted, conjured that my eardrums shuddered vibrantly to my labyrinth, my innermost vestibular and cochlea, plunging grimly into my cerebrum. I lusted to release the sharp screams, the madness, and the degree of impaling and intolerable horror from which the most daring imaginations must recoil. Upon this thought, the gravity lifted and seized to paralyse my body until I found myself emerging from unconsciousness.

I could not at once gain a proper position of my sensibilities holding the continual state of my brain and quivering nerves, upon the shuddering of my flesh. And to be at my full control, I sat erect upon my bed and stared around a couple of times though the dim and dull illuminations from the gazing window allowed only a part of the room to be somewhat seen even so not totally. I knew not what aroused me from slumber, a voice of indeed a strange familiarity.

At this times, we tend to refer to a profile of a more definitive title as an explanation to this logic 'higher functions' that interaction between our limbic system and the cortex 'highly active' during REM sleep, despite the fact that most external stimulation is cut off. In accord with the *activation-synthesis model,* dreams, a result of our mind interpreting the 'random' and unregulated process of sleep as if they were real events.

Indeed but this what I heard to the sensory coil in my brain was real to be distinguished from dreams for it shrieked my damn spirit as I recall the exact utterances. "Get thee up, I say wake, Father. How canst thou tranquilly sleep?" Thrice and not less! The sounds of these words were a shutter to ones spirit to be loosely lost without much ado. Like the sharp kind of feeling at the sight of blood. I could recall to mind neither period which I'd fall to the trance nor locality to which I then lay while I remained motionless. The night of the next day, fatigue induced me to remain prostrate upon my bed till I slumbered.

At about 12:45 a.m., the grotesque occurred without my recognisance, to which brought a deadly novo over my spirit for the second time, the impatient jeering voice now more audibly. "Get thee up, I say wake, Father, good morrow." I could not summon the boldness to move, I dared not make any effort to satisfy me of my fate, I kept silent and still. The voice to whom it spoke to proceeded relentlessly familiar words with a pugnacity of attention.

Light, icy touch tranquilly stroking back my hair like a child. "Sleep dwell upon thine eyes, peace on thy breast. Hence will I to my ghostly father's cell, his help to crave, and my dear nap to tell." The extent of these species of extreme lethargies had suppressed beyond a paralytic shock of the nerves and blood raging intolerant from the temples to the heart as I entered deeper into a series of elaborate precautions. This certainly was not a dream, for I was fully awake and aware. In sudden courage, I sat erect as if waking from a prolonged nightmare. The darkness suppressed in total blackness, I failed to take notice of the figure which had aroused me in the innumerable shadows of gloom and fear. I shuddered, my teeth chattered as I dared speak, "Who I demand art thou? Unveil!" but no response, total silence.

I left in liberty my mind to configure the state. This event for me was terribly adapted, the rigid embrace of the haunted rectory, the blackness of the absolute night, the sudden silence like the sea overwhelms, the endurable oppression of the lungs, and the unseen but palpable presence of a being. All was a rapturous astonishment, provokingly driven to be the eeriest of cowards. I broke into prayer and grew confoundedly mad.

Our father which art in heaven,
hallowed be thy name. Thy kindom come.
Thy will be done on earth as it is in heaven...

There had my incantations seize as a response thus evoked. "'Tis I, 'tis e'er I father that comes to thee." But again, I saw nobody to which it spoke, to say no mouth from which the voice emerged in the thin air. I proceeded now more madly and loudly than the first.

> Give us this day our daily bread; and forgive
> us our debts, as we forgive our debtors
> And lead us not into temptation, but
> deliver us from evil…
> —*The Geneva Bible (1602)*

Once more was the interruption, more vividly spoken. "Oh, ghostly father o' mine, apace thou forgets, yet 'tis thou consented to marry us today." This time I seized and rose up. Indeed, I recalled this date a year before. The date at which I wedded the late Romeo and his lady Juliet. I felt a sudden span of guilt and confusion for not being in the position to recall this knowledge. But how, could it really have been him, my dear boy? Certainly not, for he lived not partially but wholly as the spirit and not as man made of clay.

Forsooth the method of this ghastly occurrence could sentence one to a cardiac elapse if not well perceived. Though I knew the boy as one with many surprises to even his death, he fails to grant me a night's sleep. The clock which by this time should have moved fifteen minutes further seemed somewhat positioned at the current hour.

I searched about the room with my eyes calling out the delightful name I presumed owned the unseen words. "Romeo, is so thy voice which calls upon my name?" The voice to which it spoke to at once responded lightly and calm than before but audibly.

"'Tis I Romeo, my soul calls upon thy name." Indeed, it felt relief for I desired to hear him speak once more.

"Wherefore art thou?" I asked in the midst of nothingness.

"Hither, ghost father. Turn thee and look unto your boy," he replied as my sight followed the echo to a spectacular figure to which my eyes rested. "Holy Saint Francis!" Indeed,

I can guarantee my sight fails me not for one to conceive the idea that I am mad! Surely I was, but now no longer.

In the beginning, the image was a shimmer of mist, diffuse. Through it, the furniture and wallpaper that peeled with the raising dump became slightly out of focus like a blurry photograph. It soon congealed into a form with brilliant eyes and skin of angelic flare.

I could call to mind the death garments he kept clinging to, the tranquil innocence of his face. "Dead are you not, Romeo? For it must be artificial insomnia from a mocking nightmare… Oh, is so the case that proves me a meek slave? Oh, I fear…" in a sharper tone, suppressing impatience yet kindly, he interrupted. Now rushing closer to where I remained rooted with the urge to pursue me.

"Fear me not, ghost father. 'Tis I Romeo. A man or spirit, my name still the same," said he that felt like a partial evanescent achievement yet a mystery of vivid amazement to be comprehended.

In most cases, some unseen mysterious principles can at times be regarded as extremely difficult to understand and accept like this event. In the logic, normal world we perceive such as phenomena described widely in folklore and non-scientific bodies of knowledge. The existence within these contexts is explained to lie beyond normal experience. The spectacular magnificence proceeding before me was indeed the ghost of Romeo, best thought of as a subset of pseudoscience. To anybody's assumption about this and many extrasensory perceptions would be listed as a phantasm of a paranormal character.

The truth was indeed stranger than the fantasy that demanded attendance. For what reason would Romeo appear to only I, an old man who knows no more than God and plants. Strangely, he had a family and in-laws who made peace yet he proceeded to neither. Nevertheless, his face wore an agonising mask of a lost soul and it came to my recognition a similar expression the boy would make at the absence of his beloved Juliet. "Why do you seek me this night? Had thee not been correctly laid to rest? Beshrew me if so," I questioned, for he was buried within descent haste alongside his beloved at a cemetery well prepared by the two families.

The boy elaborated the look on his peace-deprived face. "My heart's dear love, ghost father." He seized at that statement and said nothing more of concern but by those utterances, the puzzle became a perfect fit, a precise idea of the referred. I never yet knew love would transcend so deep to wake a dead spirit.

"What of Juliet, how does she fair?" I asked, unconsciously provoking the raging impatience suppressing the spirit. Yet, he did not derail to speak the anguish though not instantly like I had expected, instead, he pursued to take a different course from that of the room. Its warmth and tenderness provided by the church, the serenity, tranquillity of the environment.

"Follow me into the outer night, and let me unfold to thee the sad solemn slumber in my grave," he said with extreme agitation and restlessness.

This situation in no whatsoever way offers options to retreat from this, yet again, a burning curiosity. I proceeded behind the ghost who had already exited the building with extreme precautions. The dreary night was bleak though the air scented pure and fresh to a certain locality. Everything seemed quieter, almost muffled in the vast expanse of the jet-black sky. The stars above shone all night for the nocturnal dwellers basking within the serenity. This was, however, publicly seen in the familiar environment around the town.

As we proceeded into the cemetery, a black limousine hearse of the graveyard slowly wended its way beneath my feet, a dark, grotesque hue after the full cast of the moon and sky now freckled with fewer stars, smudging illuminations of decayed trees with rows of tombstones erect in the near silence. Only but smatterings of stubborn night owls. Gravel paths weaved through the maze of graves to which we followed.

I held upon the crucifix laid on my chest as I reeked amongst chasing shadows and thick, oppressive fog rising within the damp earth that contained the unseen but palpable presence of conqueror worms, of wandering spirits and dancing demons. Romeo's ghost halted at a well-furnished grave and knelt before the grave of his late betrothed. He looked like one who urgently needed medical attendance but was already late. I preceded closer, pity undermining my fear but the ghost restricted any further movement with the abrupt veer of his voice. "O ghost father, grief so swift to death it drifts. What thinkest thou?" I hesitated with no precise answer to his question yet he waited no further and proceeded. "Death not sweet without my lady's face as cursed foot wonders her grave all night." As he spoke, I felt a rush of reviving souls, strong gust that could sweep one off his feet. In paranoid confusion, he dashed to where I remained rooted. "Make haste! Beneath the folds art my Juliet's soul. Commend my restless soul to her if thou finds her whole."

A dark spark flashed across my conscious and my eyes became eloquent in despair as a sickening feeling emerged pervading me with the utmost vigour. I was half startled with a thorny pressure, disgust from which the world had evoked. A hypnotic sensation overwhelmed, sounds of inquisitorial voices seemed merged into one dreamy determined ham. All other sensations seemed swallowed up in a mad rushing descent sending souls to Hades. I felt light headed at the moment as my spirit engulfed into a dark void, a trance of many dreamy lethargies and nothing. A moment of what I presume felt like death though not certain.

The next time I resumed consciousness, I was lying in the streets of Verona but not necessarily as the town would be described as busy and life full, it was the exact opposite, an extinction of many things. The sky was clearly artificial and the paths stainless as no one ever walked these grounds, though I was familiar with the location which I laid upon. Some buildings away were the Capulet holdings. The urge to ask as to what reason I came here was tense but, however, curious to proceed with his quest. In the verge of silence, I could hear distraught echoes of feminine pleas and upon arrival at the Capulet's orchard was the shadow of a feminine figure behind Juliet's upper window then nothing, empty and cold as the atmosphere below. At this point, my adrenaline level was to the peak of buzzing terror signals within my body that I began to shudder, my pulsation increased and the hairs upon my body stood erect on my skin. My sensory senses had heightened ready for flight at the slightest of sound penetrating my ears.

I sorted to proceed to the church as it was referred a safe haven after such encounters. However, on arrival, was a chill and heavy coldness of my heart to learn that every motion was undoubtedly watched. I couldn't tell if the feminine figure before the altar was holy or unholy but to my poor sight was a casual trespass having unleashed a chain of horrific events beyond my imaginations. It was not until I accomplished my purpose was I in liberty to resume the earthly life. I dared speak, "Is it you? What is thy name?"

To my expectation, she spoke, though without turning to the addresser, softly yet sadly, "Juliet of the Capulet." With this response, I built the confidence to proceed.

"Wherefore is your betrothed?"

She answered, "He lays dead, many candles aligned along the grave. I too fell but confined from the wake." Now turning to me, "Why am I here, Father? What taunts me so?" Oh, it was pitiful how she questioned, yet was so sweet her voice to dethrone me from my priesthood garments.

Perchance affection so purely undiluted that explains death may not have complete suppression of both souls to part as in ordinary occasions. "Is it not for his cause you resort to such bondage sweet? Has there been such greater love between men that the heart thus decays but not the soul? Seek his for his attempt for yours has been proven." She called for the first time, then the second, now the third. I remembered the very beginning as a slow change proceeded, the rushing in of many lingering souls in exquisite elegance, aligning with gentle motions of their dancing feet upon the transformation, a designating light and sweet hypnotic music, all beauty and wine. Alas! Upon my recognition, the veer of a faithful smile upon the lips of the girl in mourning.

Like the very first sight, I recall the strange familiarity of a certain night in the meeting. "What lady is that, which doth, enrich the hand of yonder knight?" and thus strode in King Romeo towards his beloved Queen Juliet.

"'Tis I, sweet lord of mine for my dear soul still loves till now," flowed the graceful words of her tone, as if the encounter was just yesterday. Those intriguing eyes that humbled before me in a plea for the union the year before. And thus had my sleep resumed upon the bed of my rectory and to the awakening of a brighter day from what would have been perceived by anyone as my own fancies.

Chapter 8
Odds of Benevilla
'Facts of a Town'

I witnessed a strange town that chilled every fibre of my nerves, that fails to erase from my mind, that causes my beating intervals to stammer, that confines my spirit as mad.
—*Faridah Otieno*

In the morning glad, the sun thus endeavours to lit bow the day bright.
In the gloom of night the moon declares serenity of its kind, the earth emerges daily living of man and the water of the ocean,
Rivers and hidden streams unveil the treasures of the soul.
The little town's cast of beauty night and morning ruddy and radiant like the modern portrait of Petra, the extravagant sceneries of Ciudad Perdida.
Benevilla.
The strange facts of that unnoticed in my epic poetry of Benevilla. Along the tiled roads winding about, the gipsy figures of deception.
Seductive jasmines swaying with charms under their crimson velvet and lace, in a roma dance.
Eyes emerald green in thy fantasy dream, beautiful temptress that which leaves indelible marks in the hearts of men.
Hues of tortured souls crouch in the dark corners of Benevilla's streets, grandiose, vicious mortals possessed by inner demons.

I recall common beggars with drunken eyes and ragged
fawn-coloured overcoats, not at all with the portrait of pity
nor heartfelt sympathy.
Peace came not on one's aid who walked passed them in
fear of destructive plague of midnight theft.
Magnificent was the word to describe the walls, gigantic
in height and breadth that hosted stray cats within its crafts.
Over most windows extended the trellis work of aged
vines which clambered up the massy walls.
Ceiling of gloomy oak excessively lofty, vaulted and
elaborately fretted with the wildest and most grotesque
specimen of gothic.
I remained staring pensively at the empty showcase in
the repulsive clamminess of the cold, in the gloomy and
dreary grandeur of the buildings.
In my garden the memories stole Benevilla's spectacular
image. The town, a collection of gargantuan royal tombs.
And I passed with less disquietude the gigantic
sarcophagus of black granite from the tomb of kings.
Ancient spirits of gone rulers who watch the world move
on in there eternal absence.
Thou could wonder, gaze amazed by the figures of
transparent waxen hue of the graves, the creepy fogy
tombstones written names of departed beloveds.

R.I.P	R.I.P	R.I.P
Nina Kingsley	Adam Stone	Genevieve Pritchard
1864–1999	1993–2005	1891–2002

More made each passing day, cries and agony perceived
every day like the passing seasons of the angel of death.
Common thieves sneak in the ebon darkness of the night to
dig out rich men's graves, rob the dead and make profit,
haunted wealth, poisoned gold and silver.

Beautiful springs, waterfalls of diamonds, reflections beneath it sea secrets. Untold stories never spoken of.
The vaporized purity waters expose saltiness at the bed.
I pondered in silence, in soft deceitful wails, in a provoked sense of dreary.
The liquid multicoloured eyes of Benevilla. Their startling gaze of pity, hatred, deplore, joy yet remorse.
The stranger that came in one piece, just to have a pick of Benevilla, to ink the incredible, the difference of yonder.
Yes, I, in my epic poetry of Benevilla. I rendered to write in haste of that I had seen in the shadows.
Those eyes confronting my window, those thiefty beggars scathing about my midst, those ghosts
Oh! The terror, the fright and torture.
The succubus dancing about my head with seductive tones like the air of Sodom. Their ruby, magenta, indigo, and warm yellow scarfs rubbing against my flesh.
A bounden slave in the trammels of passions and conscious possessions.
Oh! No longer could endure the lonely desolation of my dwelling in the dim decaying town. Profound bleeding that drew upon the walls.
The smell of liquor that perforated the atmosphere with drunkenness.
Sounds of bottles hit and break, others roll and one seize at my feet showing off the transparency, the night stars and morning sun illuminating its mould.
Powerful reflections that it drew from the scene, barks of laughter and fistfights from raging drunken lads, sharp casted eyes upon another.
But yet in the day could rise its difference, the remarkable outstanding sights and smiles. Benevilla.
I made sure to outstretch the facts, missing not at all one in my short existence yonder.
And until I completed that I intended in my collections of tales,

The Odds of Benevilla.

Chapter 9
The Confession
'Confessions of a Superior'

There are two kinds of pride, both good and bad. 'Good pride' represents our dignity and self-respect. 'Bad pride' is the deadly sin of superiority that reeks of conceit and arrogance.
—John C. Maxwell

Bless me, Father, for I have sinned. For years, it has been that I last confessed, for a lifetime it has been that I conspired to writhe in the unjust, the unforgiving to the might of men, the unfriendly to nobles. I rebuked standing against my demons thus I have encountered no short of those who have presumed to speak of my evil, my awful schemes to become king. Since birth, I was hated by my father, turned into a monster by Mother. For I felt my plea for love drain to insufferable gloom that consumed me to the darkest parts of my being. Life for me had been no occasion of joy, summoned by day and night the conflicting regime in my trodden path until to that one being I vowed to love. Her kind was rare, the most exquisite to the sight of all men but in my unavoidable charms she fell deeply in love. I desired to have avoided the instant we set eyes, at that moment we kissed behind the walls of fate. However, for a reason, it happened still.

That which damned her to my ruthless fate, true it is to say that I did love her. The pure angelic gaze from her eyes inspired me to stare deeper to the depth of her soul, the rose-red expression of her puffy lips lured me to kiss her passionately. She could capture sunlight with the tresses of her red hair. My fears to have not satisfied her were absurd.

How we desired to be together truly, our bond uniquely vulnerable.

That what was yet to come veered like an apocalypse raving about our midst. That day I presumed to have seen deceit in her eyes, her long-term love changing to irreversible hate. The gift of intimacy reversed to the gift of betrayal because of that done by my selfish brute of a mother. Her pledge to see me unhappy, unsuccessful took effect as I listened to the words of my beloved Adora screwing my innermost ears. Her sight of me for the long while she fancied not seeing; a cruel, wretched thing, pathetic, unworthy of anyone's love.

How the world loathed me drew a serpent on the pure sheet. I thought not twice of that I did after; each day drew further away from humanity. In a fit of revoking rage of that, I lost control drove me to kill the one who bore me life, crippled me to become a dauntless serpent yet I needed not to regret, not even if the memory would haunt me for a thousand years. I hurried from the land, love failed me to a new one for a fresh beginning. Hoping to find fortune, adventure. Durham England, a quite captivating place with the most stunning city panoramas in Europe. Winding, cobbled streets and a prominent peninsula crowned with the dramatic cathedral and castle of Romanesque architecture in the British Isles. *Remarkable,* thought I, *at last thrilling for the while in its comfort.*

More so, the life of a common man in paradise seemed not to satisfy my needs. I was not content by that life offered by day. Power tagged my spirit, strained by the purpose of my life to become king. The sweet feeling of ruling an entire species drove the mortal soul further apart. Declarer of everything where men pledge their allegiance before thee, the taste of expensive wine from an epic city, adorations, honours, and everlasting fame. It indeed could be uniquely exquisite. As I thought, staring at a mirror the reflection ought not to follow the figure before but instead the figure to be.

And in the flick of time, I became part of a council to which I claimed my ruling, whatever scraps I left the rest would pick from it. What did I have to lose, nothing. At least I had failures. I failed as a son, a friend and a man. But this I could show at all no portrait of pity to none of those who agreed not to my terms with a bit of loyalty and sacrifice. They would vow to lift their usefulness.

I lit bow a new community on the verge of time with the claimed intentions of prosperity and satisfaction with me as king. With all honesty, I unauthorised unsuitable behaviour that rather seemed to irritate my gut, that I inclined to be a scrutinise of my authority. Punishable with an inhuman capacity of cruelty. That I distaste was pure betrayal covered in whatever lays enveloping traitors. Ridiculous crews of petty thieves (bribers), grandiose adults whom to their improper believe children are savages, heavy unworthy burdens.

Many sniffed at the entrails of their own blood, slaughtered and dammed as punishment for violation of rules and the war grew thicker. That sounded more like that the mirror would be shown. From the heart of many whisperers, I tended to read the possible remarks of my nature to be described as one indifferent from brutality. A sickening of the heart I desired to long forget, overthrow with time and fancies. Those confronting eyes, others of pity which I disliked unveiled the possibility of lonesome hidden by cruelty. Everything I experienced during my growth drew me to respond respectively to the harsh unfair world.

And so I watered it in blood, rage. Beyond the fear and fame of that, I demanded thus these living nightmares pursued my dreams relentlessly. As I lay asleep by night in the dark and Barisal portrait of my room, I endured to see true blood that flowed my veins, I failed not to mind see the torture of that I conspired against my own blood, the cursing voice of my father, deadly burthen of my mother hovering. How I felt the grotesque quick approaching to consume me more. I quite did dream further the night and thought deeper the day of the momentum put to dagger me by they who loathed me with malicious insights.

Yet furthermore, in that dark, I well viewed the beast invading my being, disgust and disdain from the sight of all, dreary scars of my childhood manifesting in nightmares. Truthfully I learnt to embrace my demons; most bloody heartless pestilent mortals could incline to have for a king. Why was it that none could see the good I did, yet underneath the toxin was something good. Poor, helpless widows condemned the event to which I slew the heads of their drunken brutes of husbands who did no good to them but monstrosity. Similar to the rest of ungrateful beings.

Losing love had I, that which defined me human still. I was now convinced that not in all cases would true love transcend blood. For this and more, I carried enemies, none to call a friend in the face of the earth since the first and final I did once considered to be so, but now no more. Adora.

My visions to imagine she moved on powered the wrath, the portal I hath thrown. And in my reign love was a rule, an order not to exist. Not to me, not to another thus was a desperate foolish thing to engage in so. To be young and in love was very tragic, if not both happening to fight each other eventually due to my influence then one would give free consent to be executed in devotion to another. How I hated the sight of that I never was free to possess my entire life, love. Born a bounden slave in the trammels of wickedness and self-distaste for I grew fond of the thought of worthlessness, a burden in the lives of many, believed to be a curse.

Beneath the boldness and deceitful smiles, I lay before the crowd under my rule yet inside me reigned violence, piercing fears of that my descendants would learn of me. Those words of pure hatred and shame demonstrating exactly the type of father I would be. A monster, grandiose beast with the utmost amount of devious wits.

Without principles, I vowed to be at my worst behaviour. Enslaved men to cast my plots, compelled women to mend my brokenness and yet all the more broken I configured doing so. But why reveal my weakness that concerned them not, why bother to show mercy, forgiveness yet I was never forgiven, never shown heartfelt sympathy, chained to certain fits of hunger that not even I can contemplate. There was no name for it but only a disease that grew upon me. It makes me an abomination, cursed that needed absolution. That surface grew clearer by day, by night, by seasons, decades that I needed no more redemption.

The fragments piled with time to torments that did not frighten me, pretended to be that which truly I was not. No one I tell you was as broken, as tormented and hideous like I until I was left with no choice but to enjoy the ecstasy. Could I flee? No. To whichever part of the world it would be, everything turned from me. Petty thieves roaming the streets pickpocketing all that passed by, cold murderers hanging young children and women, kidnappers in narrow subways were placed far from reference.

I not at all crept into people's wallets; I crept and plucked their pride and innocence. Neither did I kill nor hide instead killed and showcased in absolute confidence. Nor did I kidnap for ransom, I took for pleasure and personal gain till one proved no more useful. Religious souls approached in many occasions dressed in robes and with all religious equipment claiming the head needed an exorcism to make peace with his demons. Did I fragile from this? No, certainly not. Their plight was to follow and not conspire to cure the rebelling spirit from bizarre. Not do I literally mean alive with conscious but candles flickered in fright at my approach, cold and dull, pallid surrounding was what my eye fancied if not true.

Whoever stood bold enough to confront saw their last, thrown at the edge of a tall wall by my own hands one after the other in a row. It was sad that from the countless a few survived, escaped from my domain with loses. Soon after, I tried to change, forced myself to bend low to the will of men but all in vain like before, like the past declared to weakness by my father despite catching a worthy hunt. I failed the more to please those under and around me thus inflicted them all the more, relentlessly shadowing their paths. Well aware did I become that I would fall in countless ways to which I rebuked aggressively as a superior even if so meant turning the territory to a burrow rife with mutual enemies.

I needed alliances, bought a few with promised benefits others with threats. Each had ideas; engaging in treaties that later proved otherwise. The result was the death of an entire cabinet and formation of new weaker parties in comparison to I. Oh! Deeply I was termed as the devil in disguise, with irresistible charms that made many women become unfaithful to their husbands. Strongly induced with the words of my mouth and lust in my touch. They showed in plenty, young maidens, woes, wives, and young mothers all at a go. The portrait of my skin lured them to touch me, the colour of my eyes summoned them before me like puppets just to stare, a smile from my lips anchored their hearts to fall in their knees at my feet, and the fragrance from my body poisoned their souls to deceive their men.

Yet I failed not to mind their lust to which I gave freely but not did I ever anticipate to commit my heart to either but the one to whom I long lost. The consequences to love taught me not to attempt once more. For what use would it be? Conjuring the same heartbreak? Cropping into the same devastation of love based wickedness? The words of a hundred deaths? If you presume that by Adora's return, I would lighten the wrath I cannot tell for it was pure fantasy and nothing more. She was perfect just as she was, she did not deserve me in the first place. I only inspired her with sorrow.

To the high most part of sin a mortal can engage mine had suppressed outstandingly, not a number in the commandment did I fail to commit and more. Till no more do I wish to hunger for days, perish without notice from the face of the earth but before so, it was my desire to confess and seek refuge. Pardon me for my sins, I never meant it, certainly not for it saddens me so. Lord have mercy on me.

Chapter 10
The Casket of John Cooper
'Tale of Grim Death'

Death whispers, darkness heeds, immortal savagery…

The day's task had come to a close as Mr Milles, a potter, retired after a day of quite a good profit in his pottery business. Sold about 50 pots to his customers who I can well describe being utterly pleased by his beautifully patterned and strong contained pots. Nothing I tell you would seem to withdraw the joy drawn from his passion, confidently making his way home to share the excitement with his noble family. At the verge of Mr Milles' journey, a breathtaking sight arrested his attention. The face of his map drew him to the old border ridge 50 metres from the lone road eastwards beneath some tall dense trees. Beneath its folds laid a casket that was provokingly altering. The golden lining of its sides glowed exquisitely, rather charming to its beholder like Mr Milles and the rest of it was snow white, stainless, portraying not at all a trace of dirt, mud or gravel. *Who must have left this here and why?* thought Mr Milles, *Has he no respect for the dead?* The potter was not convinced to leave it at that, least afraid of the horror he was subjecting himself to.

In boldness, Mr Milles attempted to lift its top but in vain. It was entirely sealed and the weight of the casket was considerably heavy. To anyone's certain assumption, it could be proof that indeed there was a body existing inside the carpentry. This concluded to the potter's conscious that a funeral must have been left undone, a half burial. "Remarkable," uttered him, deeply wishing that someone was with him at the scene to tell the statement. Indeed remarkable but in a somewhat ghastly endeavour.

The night was fast approaching untimely and Mr Milles veered deep into his thoughts for a silent and quick solution. He was a quite curious collector, finding every possible means to preserve his significant finding until further research. He knew not what to do at the moment but at least knew where to drag and hide the casket for the night. Nearby, he figured out an old ruin, a little dirty hall with blood-coloured panes for a place picked up from abandonment. It was once a church construction established by a rich fellow and later declined after he relocated to France two years ago. Mr Milles broke off and at the sunset of day next, he once more returned. With him this time was two gents Dr Riley and Mr Grey Fretcher, a well-known carpenter in the town as well. Both had been good friends with Mr Milles for a long time and sure it was that he must have mentioned the grotesque encounter to them of what he witnessed the previous evening.

This time, however, their approach was in a later hour of the ageing night, about 9:30 p.m. It was no bother to meet at such devious time since none of the three would rise early to engage in their careers, it being a Sabbath. Anyone who would have spotted them would assume a grim plot. At the old ruin, the spectral image laid on the arrangement of granitic rocks that perused to fill Dr Riley and Mr Fretcher with an excited disgust as they apparently stared with a strange glance. Dumbfounded, unable to comprehend the circumstances and speculations sieged before them. *This is incredibly grim*, thought Dr Riley evoking a horrid feeling within him with the additional fact of viewing such at this time of night. With questioning lips, he turned to Mr Milles who no longer portrayed surprise since he witnessed casket before. Himself being the one who provided shelter for it. "And what the bloody hell is this?" asked he. But what answer could Mr Milles have to give, nothing explainable to be mentioned but only gaze in horrid amazement.

However, the carpenter was certain about one thing. The white casket was of his work. "My most significant piece of carpentry," he uttered as if possessed by the beautiful coffin.

Mr Milles now interested, "Your craft. Is it you say?"

"Indeed, I did and if I can confidently recall, I sold the coffin two weeks ago to a stranger," explained Mr Fretcher.

"A stranger?" whispered Dr Riley as if in fear to wake the dead inside the coffin.

"Might he have said something unrelated?" added Mr Milles. There drew silence for a short while as the carpenter, Mr Fretcher sank deeper into his thoughts. The air outside and in was biting cold and air damp. It could be absolutely seen that the three gents were shivering but what they were succumbed to overwhelmed them to feel no breeze tingling their skin.

It was no matter for the carpenter to speak about it and so he proceeded to answer Mr Milles' curious question.

"Yes, in fact, the stranger spoke of a rare death of his old acquaintance. Well, rare in this town about a dark murder of Mr John Cooper a few weeks back."

The say of that name, John Cooper startled Mr Milles and to reassure the statement of that Mr Fretcher spoke of, he asked, "John Cooper, are you absolute was the name?"

"Very correct, Milles, a merchant he was known as I believe." The potter felt a spirit of guilt pervading him for not being in possession of this knowledge. He once knew him though, the merchant was a silent and secretive one yet he failed to know of his murder.

A noble British subject stripped down and later drowned in a river. His body then found laid on the banks by some townsmen but too late to revive him, in which of these cases is said 90 per cent of drowning patients cannot be revived successfully or if otherwise a secondary drowning far much biologically intolerable for the human respiratory organs. On the surface of things, it was inclined to the opinion that the poor fellow was dead, not only physically but clinically proved to no longer exist. A calculated hour of death 1:34 a.m. of 3rd March 2005.

That was all Mr Fretcher knew and not more than that. All the three men concluded the possibility of John Cooper's corpse laying stiff inside the casket. The idea presented clearly in the revision of the story. Dr Riley was afraid wishing he knew nothing at this entire queer and eccentric situation that was hard to please him. "We must find means to open this thing," Mr Miles suggested. He was a bold and robust man. "If our speculations are indeed correct before we take action," he added.

"No! This should be made known to the law," said the doctor in utmost fear.

Mr Milles possessing him of his arm, "You will do no such thing until we unseal the box," said he. Tension grew in the shelter as the two crossed path over the casket. By then the grey light was coming between the midnight and morning, and thunder was holding up in the thick oppressive air as if the rains were approaching.

Suddenly their conversations were constrained to a pause in the middle of this philosophy and their attention arrested in disapprobation and surprise when the casket flung open at both the head and foot without a handful force. Finally, the latter lusted to peep in. There was nothing, a dark black entity protruded like an endless hole at the base of the coffin, sickening, intolerant to the blood, quiet, dark and ugly to the eyes, an eerie, devious void. "Oh, dear," Dr Riley whispered in fright as they watched a ghastly scene of evil fancies. There was profound bleeding from inside that smeared spontaneously outside the walls of the casket forming devious stains of blood on the white colouring. The stream of blood seemed to have a direction of flow as it rushed under the three men's shoes and spreading itself vastly around the floor and the casket. In less than five minutes, the casket was crimson from snow white. No trace of the white purity was left shouting.

There was a lot of unsuitable phantasms bizarre, something of the terrible evoking like a multitude of nightmares writhing in and about. The three fancied to know what struck them first, yet to know what came next in the affair of the sort. Hollow, detestable tones from a villainous mouth and a strong suffocating odour assailed their nostrils. Almost immediately from the brazen lungs of the voice inside the box rose a dreary magnificent that outraged loud and clear at a moment.

There was a shudder of horror and distaste as the gents listened unavoidably to this extravagant discourse. "Never in my years as a doctor have I encountered such," uttered Dr Riley.

"Quite horrid, indeed," added Mr Fretcher. The potter on his side was thrown into a tale that presented difficulty to adhere, he wished to betake in himself that everything was a contemptible falsehood. It then deteriorated to a low feeble yet audible pestilent voice at the assembly.

A ghostly rhythm saturated the air addressing that whom he spoke to, "Yes, yes, I am horridly magnificent." Mr Fretcher staggered back in absolute fright at the pestilent echo of his words from the casket. Mr Milles had failed to correspond with the strange facts, but he tried hard to make familiar the voice and dared ask just to hear it once more. "Are you dead?" But no response. He pursued to ask once more now more audibly and disturbed. The potter disliked silence, it justified ignorance and impoliteness.

"Yes, I am not alive," the voice responded.

"Can it be so?" Milles thought aloud to himself, the faded tone remarking relentlessly in his head. Indeed, for a keen listener, the tone could be correct to incline that it was the late merchant. "They say you were murdered, why must you when you ought to be dead?" asked he.

"I am dead, I am not alive," repeated the feeble sound once more. Dr Riley wished this man never died, he had a mystery in him.

"This is nonsense, I am out of here," he whispered in Mr Mille's ear who remained standing there bewildered until the remark and seized him before he took off in an errant.

The pestilent sight had been so hideous in a vague, unpleasant fashion enough to drive any man mad out of his wits. The underlying unseen spirit was too much for a mere mortal to take, too many conjectures born in one's head. If only it was a bit more pleasant like a heavenly angel from a noble earthly background like the biblical point of view about the holy resurrection. Not at all was the revelation of this figure in terms with goodness. The river of blood, the horror of the voice, the fantasy of living death. Why couldn't the devious ghost as it claimed to be seek after the murderers who pursued him to such a state of an evil clown? "Why do you disturb my peace?" once again the voice to whom it spoke to rose. His peace he had uttered out of its hiding den of no possible existence, surely he had no peace or else he could be making better use of his immortal life sailing in the shores of paradise in the afterlife.

As a couple of literary words cannot explain or justify this at the presence of the jury. Like one could surface the facts as a sorcery. Upon these facts, the three gentlemen found themselves into such a predicament. Without further utterances in the supreme stillness and total silence, rare dizziness was felt, a feeling of fatigue and drunkenness. Within their knees jerk of endurable heaviness and weakness thus in a heap collapsed in a fainted story. After uncertain seconds, minutes, or hours of unconsciousness Mr Milles flipped and back his eyes unable yet to discern distinct sounds, no equilibrium and confusion. The second to arouse from slumber was Mr Fretcher with similar madding rush conjuring in his mind. The third was one known for oversleeping which maintained his household a nagging wife, Dr Riley who not like the rest jerked up as someone waking from a prolonged nightmare frantic and yelling.

Upon such a scenario were a total bizarre connection of the previous state and the current circumstance never in the lives of the three suppressed. They lasted to release sharp screams as they were at length bounded in the utmost believed terror. Summoned before a jury in the skirts of an untamed dimension of many lingering spirits. Before them aligned black candles with a burning flame of red, black-robed insignificant judges and amongst one who sat the mad dead man. The first expression was to assume the three gentlemen were influenced into the mind of a damned spirit or to say a restless dead man's mind they could not withdraw.

They gave the first glance to Dr Riley and the dead man stated what a riddle seemed. "One who indeed is a doctor is wiser than three minds of geniuses put together to solve a puzzle for the lives of all three lay upon your creativity to keep the heart in the beat." A misty vapour wended beneath the doctor as the dead one proceeded. "What lives in its own substance and dies when it devours itself?" as he left Dr Riley to contemplate, he proceeded to the carpenter Mr Fretcher. "Your art is indeed splendid but a too soon declaration of one's death who lay in it. Help me this puzzle for I am none with such skill. The creator needs it not, the buyer gives it a scowl, and the receiver has no knowledge he shall use. What is it?"

Dr Riley in an unconscious frustration uttered, "Spirit that knows no rest is the answer! Release me, I demand! Let I attend to the living."

The gaze of Mr Fretcher was that less of aggression but utmost confusion. "Scarps of my crafted tools is the answer that holds no worth to the living but only left to be wafted with the wind."

The latter writhed with a deadly locution, a scowl with every utterance of a letter with no succession of the sound as if not meant to be revealed whatsoever. And with each for a wrong answer took a life. Mr Milles had no power to whatsoever plea as he was forced to witness the sad means to an end of his two friends. A burning candle was the absolute answer to Dr Riley's puzzle and thus consumed with every bit of flame. The other answer to Mr Fretcher was a coffin and was consumed by a deathly wind to a vapour of vigil ash and upon their fainted bodies back at the old ruin just but now desiccating corpses unable to retrieve their souls.

He was now alone, the very nerve in his body tempting to a spat about, his heart in a beating fiery that threatened to tear out his ribs and his spirit faint in a persistent coldness and chilliness. And so the final riddle was presented, "I never was, am meant to be, none has kept yet the sight of me, nor ever will. And yet I am the confidence of all to live and breathe on this terrestrial ball."

At first, Mr Milles was subdued to total stillness with thoughts clashing within his head, spinning about creating more hallucination of the horror. He witnessed the change of events; whispers of the hungry spirits now vivid, the candles aligned on the table melting away profusely to the descent of blood forms like he had seen before with the casket, many blurry figures as he pondered, plunging deeper into his thoughts for the absolute answer to this riddle. And their heads became a fire breathing skulls and their robes parasitic conjuring smoky hues ready to devour upon their still target. Their sharp claws like a vulture's.

Thus within those eyes, Mr Milles configured the puzzle, the many expressions of regret John Cooper had drawn upon him in a tangled mess. That cold waft of bitterness he swept across to hide away the shame of forever in the desiccated state, and no longer as man to see the many tidings every day brought. The thought of his own death was antagonising to his spirit, his unfair judgment he carries on to others so they might not see the sun as he does, the dawn of a new day. "Tomorrow! Tomorrow!" Mr Milles, at last, yelled out and for a short while was total silence.

"Yes indeed! That what a dead spirit can never yet see that makes him haunt the living sick unto death!"

In the declaration of this answer, the latter parading before the potter washed from the gothic decorations of their dimension and upon the face of the late merchant was that of dire depression, sad and utmost lonely. To some extent, he would be pitied. As he faded the last of him, Mr Milles would see was the liquid eyes he swore never to forget. And in a flash, he was yet to imagine his body lying upon the ruin woke from slumber to a bright sunny tomorrow. The time was now 9:00 a.m. and evidence of the casket was no longer in sight. He viewed beside the corpses of his late allies, and his last resort was to bitterly weep and as he did, he drew in his mind those liquid eyes, the liquid eyes of John Cooper.

Chapter 11
Guilt of Killing
'A Murder Case'

Dissociated, I follow this body in its reckless haste.
—*Taylor Patton*

Blood smell smeared on my hands, filled my heart with guilty venom and so did the horror come creeping on the death situation. Like chasing shadows silently cropping the bits of an old innocent life. The old lady was already dead in the face of society. She had already suffered the loneliness life left her with. Lived with no husband nor children for twenty years. All the old lady could grasp was a pot of gruel in a blue moon. What was the point of living? I made no mistake of ending all her deplore.

That night was silent, only the mere hooting of owls broke the silence at a distance. The thought of what lurked in the dark was grotesque, but for me, it was rather the best time for execution. Trees swayed relentlessly with the passing winds in whispers and the wet moat grass stood firm in its roots waiting to be sprinkled by blood from the merciless act. I pushed open the door that could hardly prevent a rodent from penetrating in the hut. I carried a knife which I slid in my back pocket. Steadily and carefully, I moved near to avoid making a waking sound like a thief optimistic of stealing a life. And there she was peaceful on her bed of reeds. Broken and demined by life yet not neither even a gang of thieves nor would whispers of the crickets seem to disturb her sleep.

I tilted my head closer to her wrinkled dry face. Her breath felt warm in the cold atmosphere and the fragrance from her skin smelled like lavender, a quite pleasant smell not worth poor flesh. "Why should you live this hostile life? That has been no good to you. Here you have only planted barren seeds that you dearly wished would grow into roses, red as blood," I gently whispered, allowing my word to stream down her earlobe as I continued. "But old grandma, in them only flourished choking thorns that have pricked you over and over."

I drew the blade from my pocket and raised it. I then plunged it directly into her chest and blood came oozing like a spring. A heavy thunder struck and large drops of rain hit the earth. Her blood rushed down under my boots. There was no struggle, no grasping for cusps of breath. It was that easy sucking the life out of the old lady like she expected to perish from the living world. Not even the expression of her face changed, now much clear, and her body relaxed. I immediately covered her with palm leaves and flee from the hut.

The rain had become too strong to spare neither any walking pedestrian from a killing cold nor a driver from tragedy. At the moment, it felt beautiful doing it, a deletion of all dark memories from an old hag. I barely felt the guilt, but as I walked on the murky, wet street it became clearer in my head that the murdered blood was soaking my palms. Terrors suddenly span my nerves. I saw her rage bethrow me, seizing me from freedom with her blood. I yelled trying to rub off the bloodstains on my blouse.

The crystal, clear rainwater reflected the face of the dead peasant. Pale and tearless in the moonlight. "Would you care to join me?" a faint voice spoke from the grey clouds. I coiled my body on the pathway.

"No, you are wrong, old woman!" I yelled, confronting her relentless voice. "I have a story to tell. How I saved you from your sorrows, emptied into a pit of forever tears. I tell you, I tell you, you are dead," I continued. Now it became a haunted story. This deed pressed me and darkness consumed me that instant.

I realised that I rendered a restless ghost that I had the chance to avoid. But no, I had to console myself. It was the cruel world that murdered the old lady. I seemed to have seen a dark edge, that voice telling me to join her. A ghost that made the face of reality vanish from my sight. All my eyes would see is illusions. Cold intriguing words of guilt streamed down my earlobe. I put myself together and lifted from the sidewalk. I strode on alone all the way home, headed straight upstairs to my bedroom and stripped the bloody blouse from my body.

Whatever happened that night would live to be my own secret. Just before the thought of throwing myself in bed, I slithered exhaustively to my window and swung it open. The cold night breeze came rushing through my skin which made me slightly shiver. I looked down into the streets below. There were no signs of life, just as quiet as a graveyard. It felt like the world stood since the incident. But aside the cool breeze I felt something trickling down my spine like sweat. Fear struck me abruptly when I turned and stared back into the room.

Before me, a ghastly figure approached. It only took me a glimpse to recognise the bleeding wound on its chest and the unhealthy look on its face. "You are dead!" I shouted in terror but she only drew closer and the smell of death came dashing ahead. Her movements were smoky. The walls of my room narrated my guilt as I stood there confused to the point of insanity.

"Stop fooling yourself and live by the consequences of your act." These words repeated themselves like numerous tormenting echoes in my ears. Finally, I could take it no longer; my heart grew dark and as cold as frost. I turned back to face the night, it was the only way to escape this as it was jumping out the window. As I dived into the dark night, the guilt journeyed through the air with the wind.

CPSIA information can be obtained
at www.ICGtesting.com
Printed in the USA
LVHW020834010719
622841LV00021B/1015